Christina's Kite
and
Other Stories

by
ENID BLYTON

Illustrated by
Dudley Wynne

AWARD PUBLICATIONS

For further information on Enid Blyton please contact www.blyton.com

ISBN 0-86163-613-9

Text copyright © The Enid Blyton Company

Illustrations copyright © 1994 Award Publications Limited

Enid Blyton's signature is a trademark of The Enid Blyton Company

This edition entitled *Christina's Kite and Other Stories* published by permission of The Enid Blyton Company

First published 1994
8th impression 2001

Published by Award Publications Limited,
27 Longford Street, London NW1 3DZ

Printed in Hungary

CONTENTS

Christina's Kite

When Christina was nine, she had a lovely kite given to her for her birthday. It was a big one, and it had the face of a cat painted on it. Christina was very pleased with it.

"I've never had a kite before," she said. "Never! This is a beauty. And oh, what a fine tail it has!"

The kite was red and yellow, and it had a tail of brightly-coloured paper. With it had come a big ball of string.

"And it's a fine windy day too!" said Christina. "So it will be just right to fly the kite this morning."

She took it to the hillside, where the wind was very strong. Alan, Mary, George, and Tom saw her carrying it.

"Many happy returns of the day,"

said Mary. "I say! Is that one of your presents? Can we come and help you to fly it?"

"No," said Christina, who was very bad at sharing her things with others. "I want to fly it all by myself. You're not to come with me."

"You're a selfish girl," said George. "You wouldn't let us have a ride on your bicycle the other day, and you wouldn't let us have a try at spinning your top."

Christina didn't say anything. She turned her back on the others and went on by herself. The others stared after her, and then went on into the fields to play Catch.

Christina unwound a great deal of string. She shook out the kite's tail. She threw it up into the strong wind. It flew high at once. Oh, it was a fine kite pulling strongly at the string, longing to go higher and higher and higher!

"You're a splendid kite!" called Christina joyfully as she watched it climbing into the sky. "You will soon have used all my string!"

She began to run with the kite, because it pulled so hard – and suddenly she stepped into a rabbit-hole, twisted her ankle, and fell down flat!

"Oh!" cried Christina. "I've hurt my foot! Oh! I can't get up! Help! Help!"

But the wind blew her voice away, and nobody heard her. The kite pulled

hard at the string. Christina was still holding it. The kite was flying high above the field where the other children were playing. How Christina wished she had let them come with her and share the kite! Then they could have helped her.

An idea came into her head. Perhaps the *kite* could help her. She began to pull it in. At last it was lying on the grass beside her. The little girl pulled out her notebook and wrote on a page:

"I have hurt my foot. I am on the hill. Please help me. Christina."

Then she broke off the last piece of the kite's tail and tied the note there instead. She tried to throw the kite into the air, but it was difficult now she was sitting down. The wind was dropping too – but at last the kite did rise a little, and at once Christina let out some more string.

It flew into the air, but it dipped down and round every now and again

because the wind was not so strong now. Still, it flew upwards and was soon high in the air.

And now, when it dipped down, Christina did not pull at the string to make it rise up again. Instead she let the string go slack, so that the kite dipped still further. The wind dropped again – and down went the kite in great circles, dipping right to the ground.

It fell among the children, who were surprised to see it falling there. "It's Christina's kite," said Alan. "We'd better throw it up for her."

But as they were going to throw it into the wind, Mary noticed the odd bit of white paper tied to the end of the coloured tail.

"Wait a minute," she said. "What's this?" She took the note and read it. "Oh," she said, "this is a note from Christina. She's hurt her foot on the hillside. We must go and help her."

"I don't see why we should," said George. "Selfish girl! She won't let us go with her when she's got a new toy – but she wants us quickly enough when she needs help."

"Don't be mean, George," said Mary. "You needn't come if you don't want to – but I shall go, anyhow."

George went too, and the others. They soon found Christina sitting by the rabbit-hole, her face still white. She couldn't possibly walk on her hurt foot. She had twisted her ankle very badly.

They managed to get her home between them. Her mother was worried when she saw them coming,

and ran out to see what was the matter.

"Never mind, Christina," she said. "We will put a cold, wet bandage on your ankle, and the swelling will soon go down if you rest it."

"What about my birthday party?" wept poor Christina.

"Well, dear, as you didn't want anybody to your party except Daddy, Auntie, and me, it won't be much of a disappointment not to have it," said Mother, who was always feeling sad because Christina wouldn't share things with her friends.

So there was no birthday party for Christina; but later on, when her foot was better, Christina sent out invitation cards to all her friends. She had been thinking a lot whilst she had lain still with her bad ankle.

"I really *am* selfish!" thought Christina. "I never share anything with anybody – and yet I love to wheel Jenny's pram when she lets me, and I always take one of John's sweets if he offers me any. I feel ashamed of myself now. I wouldn't share my kite – and yet when the other children knew I was hurt they came running to help. I didn't deserve their kindness. But I'll make up for it now."

So she is having a lovely party now that her foot is better, and is going to share her cake and her chocolates and balloons and toys with everyone. She'll be much happier if she does, won't she?

And *next* time she flies her kite, *every*one is going with her to help. They're sure to have a fine time up on the windy hillside.

The Toy Soldier's Adventure

Once Emily and Robert took some toys out into the garden to play with them. They took the wooden soldier and the clockwork clown. They took the moneybox pig, who was quite empty, because the children had taken all their pennies out of his middle the week before to buy a present for their mother's birthday. And they took Waddle, the yellow duck whose head could twist round and round.

Now, when they went into the house again, they quite forgot to take back the moneybox pig. They left him out on the grass. But they took the wooden soldier, the clockwork clown, and the yellow duck.

When the children had gone to bed and the nursery was quite quiet, there

13

came a voice that wailed through the nursery.

"Has anyone seen my lovely, lovely sword?"

It was the wooden soldier. As soon as he had come alive that night he had found that his fine sword was missing! A wooden soldier is nothing without his sword, and he was most upset.

"We'll look around for it," said the clockwork clown. So he looked. And Waddle the duck looked, and all the dolls, both big and small. But nowhere could they find the sword of the poor wooden soldier!

"It's not among the bricks," said the clown.

"It's not in the toy station anywhere," said the yellow duck.

"It's not anywhere in the dolls' house," said the dolls, walking out of the front door in a row.

"I say!" said the clown suddenly, "where's the old moneybox pig? I haven't seen him anywhere tonight!"

"I do believe he must have been left

out in the garden!" said the duck, in alarm. "Oh dear – and he is such a timid creature! He is even scared of a spider!"

"Yes," said the big doll, "he is certainly timid. Once when a fly walked over his back he squealed out loudly and said a lion had jumped on him! Whatever shall we do? He will be so very very frightened out in the garden all by himself."

"Wooden soldier, you must go and find him," said the clockwork clown. "Soldiers are always brave."

"I don't feel brave without my sword," said the wooden soldier. "I

don't want to go. Suppose I met a cat – or even a mouse – and I hadn't got my sword to frighten it away – I should have to run away myself."

"Don't be such a coward," said the duck. "I always thought you were the bravest of us all. Go out and find the moneybox pig and bring him home, soldier."

"I feel too unhappy about my lost sword to do anything at all but wish and wish I could find it," said the soldier sulkily. "Don't bother me about fetching the pig. He's got four legs, hasn't he? Well, then, he can walk home himself."

"That's just what he won't do," said the duck. "He'll be too scared to move a step."

The wooden soldier sat down sulkily

on the brickbox, wondering where his nice sword was. But after a bit he began to think of the moneybox pig out in the dark and the cold all alone.

"I'd better go and look for him," thought the wooden soldier. "I don't like to think of him squealing out there every time a spider walks over his toes!"

So he slipped down the stairs and out the back door. He ran down the path to the place where the children had been playing that morning. He ran into a big snail and fell over. He slipped on a fat worm and sat down suddenly. It was

17

very difficult to see anything coming in the dark.

He called the moneybox pig softly.

"Pig! China Pig! Where are you?"

"Here! Here!" squealed the pig. "Oh, is that you, wooden soldier? I have nearly died of fright out here all by myself. A spider is making a web between my ears, and is tickling me dreadfully, but I can't laugh because I am too frightened. It is terrible to be tickled and not be able to laugh."

"I'm coming, moneybox pig," said the wooden soldier, and he made his way over the grass. It was very wet. The soldier got his red trousers dripping wet. He saw a big mouse looking at him with shining eyes, and he wished he had his sword to frighten it away. A mouse was very big to the little soldier.

The mouse ran away. The wooden soldier at last came up to where the pig stood in the damp grass. "Take hold of my coat," said the soldier. "I will lead you back to the nursery."

"Could you take away the spider that is spinning its web between my ears?" asked the pig. "I can't laugh yet, and it does tickle me so."

The soldier brushed away the spider, and it ran into the bushes. Then he and the pig made their way back to the nursery – but at every step the moneybox pig rattled in a most peculiar manner!

"What's the matter with your middle?" asked the wooden soldier in surprise. "Have you any pennies in you again? You do make a funny noise when you walk."

"I don't know what's inside me," said the pig mournfully. "A cheeky little pixie spoke to me this evening and popped something into my money-slit – but it wasn't money. Whatever it was makes me rattle dreadfully. I don't like it."

The pig was so glad to be back in the nursery again – and the toys laughed at him because he rattled so loudly when he moved.

"Let's see what the pixie put inside him," said the clockwork clown. So they turned him upside down and shook him till the thing that rattled slid out of the money-slit.

And what do you suppose it was! It was the wooden soldier's sword! Fancy that! It had dropped off into the grass when the children had played with him that morning! The pixie had found it as he came running by that night, and had popped the sword into the moneybox pig for mischief! And there it was, as good as ever.

"My sword, my beautiful sword!" cried the soldier in delight, buckling it on again. "Oh, how very happy I am!"

"And so am I," said the moneybox pig, standing the right way up again. "You came to find me, all in the dark and cold, soldier – and I brought you back your sword, though you didn't know it! You were kind to me, and your kindness gave back to you the sword you had lost!"

"That's *wonderful*," said the clockwork clown. And so it was.

21

A
Great Big Story

Once there was a little girl called Janet. You may know her, and if you do you will say that she is a nice, friendly, clever little girl with a smile for everyone. But just listen to what happened to her!

At the beginning of the week Janet was happy and had many friends. But at the end of the week what a difference! Poor Janet had no friends at all, she was very miserable, and she cried so much one night that her pillow was too damp to lie on.

And now let me tell you what happened.

On Monday, Janet lost her rubber, and went to tell Miss Brown. "Oh, Janet dear, what a pity!" said Miss

Brown. "You are usually such a careful little girl. You can go to my cupboard in the next room, and take a new rubber for yourself from the shelf there. Do it after school."

So at the end of the morning Janet went to the next room, opened the cupboard door, and took a new rubber off the shelf. She slipped it into her pocket.

Now who should pass by the room at that moment but Rachel. She looked in – and she saw Janet taking the rubber from the cupboard. And silly Rachel thought that Janet was taking it

23

without Miss Brown knowing. She stood and stared – and then she ran off to tell Sally.

"I say, Sally," whispered Rachel, her eyes shining, "do you know what I've just seen? I've seen Janet taking a rubber out of Miss Brown's cupboard. She thought nobody saw her! Whatever would Miss Brown say if she knew?"

"Oooh, what a bad girl Janet is!" said Sally at once. "I don't think I like her now. You know, Rachel, I shouldn't be surprised if she took a pencil too, and you didn't see her."

Well, when Sally went home from school, she walked with Jack. Jack liked Janet, and he spoke about her to Sally.

"I'm going to tea with Janet tomorrow," he said. "She's got a lovely new book she's going to show me."

"Well, I hope she didn't take it out of Miss Brown's cupboard then!" said Sally.

"Whatever do you mean?" asked Jack, surprised.

"Well didn't you know that Janet took a rubber and pencil out of Miss Brown's special cupboard – the one we are not allowed to go to?" said Sally, quite enjoying Jack's look of surprise.

"How disgusting of Janet!" said Jack. "I shan't go to tea with her. That's stealing. My mother will never let me go to tea with children like that."

So on Tuesday Jack told Janet he couldn't go to tea with her. He spoke in such a funny cold voice that Janet was quite hurt. Jack ran off before Janet could ask him why he wouldn't go to tea.

"Why did you speak to Janet in such a horrid voice?" asked Harry, in surprise.

"Because she's a little thief," said Jack. "She steals things. Sally told me."

"Gosh!" said Harry, in horror. "I never knew that before. Do you think she took that ruler of mine that I lost, Jack?"

"I shouldn't be surprised," said Jack. Harry felt quite certain then that Janet had his ruler, and he scowled at her when he met her. She was surprised and puzzled.

"Why are you frowning at Janet?" Kate asked Harry.

"Because she stole my ruler," said Harry. "She's a little thief. Didn't you know? I wouldn't be surprised if she was the one who broke that window the other day, and didn't own up."

Well, in less time than I have taken to tell you all this, the news went round the school that Janet was a bad, naughty girl who stole things, and broke windows and didn't own up, and all kinds of other things. And by the time that Friday came, poor Janet hadn't a single friend, and was dreadfully unhappy because the children treated her so unkindly. Miss Brown found her sobbing about it at the end of Friday morning.

"I'll soon find out what's the matter," she said to Janet. "It's all a silly mistake, I expect."

"I heard Kate say I was a bad, naughty girl, and that I stole," sobbed Janet. "But I never do that, truly I don't."

"Of course you don't!" said Miss Brown. "You are one of the most truthful and honest children in the class."

Well, Miss Brown asked Kate what she meant, and Kate told her that Harry had said Janet had stolen his ruler.

Then Miss Brown spoke to Harry. "Well, Jack told me that Janet was a thief, so I thought maybe she *did* take my ruler," said Harry, going red.

Then Miss Brown went to Jack, looking rather stern. Jack stammered out that Sally had told him that Janet had taken a pencil and rubber from Miss Brown's special cupboard. Miss Brown looked sterner and sterner, and called Sally up to her desk.

"Well, it was Rachel who told me," said Sally. "She said she saw Janet taking a rubber from your cupboard, Miss Brown."

"Tell Rachel to come here," said Miss Brown in rather a dreadful voice. So Rachel came, and she told how she had seen Janet taking a rubber from Miss Brown's special cupboard. "I really did see her, Miss Brown," said Rachel. "I didn't make it up."

29

"Rachel, *I* told Janet to take that rubber," said Miss Brown sternly. "She had my permission. She is a good, honest little girl, who would never dream of taking what didn't belong to her. *You* are the horrid, bad, dishonest, untruthful child – you started a little story that has grown into a Great Big Story, and gone all round the school, so that poor, innocent, kind little Janet has no friends, and is very miserable and puzzled. Please put this right at once. I am really ashamed of you!"

Rachel was dreadfully ashamed of herself. After school that afternoon she told all the others, with tears running down her cheeks, what Miss Brown had said. They listened in silence, looking very red and ashamed.

"We're all to blame," said Harry at last. "We all added to the horrid story. We all believed it. I feel dreadful. I'll never do a thing like this again. I'm going to tell Janet I'm sorry."

So they all made it up with Janet, and she smiled again. Harry took her a book she wanted. Jack lent her his new calculator. Rachel gave her a doll's hat – and everyone did their very best to make up for the wrong they had done.

Well, well – who would have thought that a Great Big Story could have come out of such a tiny thing? Really, we'll have to be very careful we never do such a thing ourselves! I *should* feel ashamed – wouldn't you?

He Couldn't
Be Trusted

"Rilloby!" called Dame Get-Along.
"Will you call at the butcher's for me
on your way down to the village and
tell him I've got my two brothers
coming to supper tonight and will he
please send up extra meat?"

"Oh yes, Dame Get-Along, with
pleasure!" said Rilloby, and he skipped
along with his basket.

But, of course, he didn't remember!
Rilloby couldn't be trusted with any
message or any job. He either forgot, or
he couldn't be bothered, or he did it so
badly that he might just as well not
have done it at all!

There was the time when a pipe
burst in Mr Doodle's bathroom, and he
leaned out of the window and yelled to

Rilloby: "Rilloby, get the plumber, quick! My pipe's burst, and I've got my thumb over the hole. Fetch him, will you?"

"Of course, of course!" cried Rilloby. But he met Winky, who had a new bicycle and said he would let him have a ride on it. He didn't get to the plumber's until hours later, and by that time the man had gone out. So poor Mister Doodle had to stand all morning in his cold bathroom with his thumb over the hole in the pipe!

"You just can't trust Rilloby," he grumbled. "He always says he'll do

this, that and the other, but he doesn't! He's not to be trusted!"

Then there was the time when Rilloby promised his next-door neighbour that he would look after his cat whilst he was away – and he forgot all about it! So when his friend came back the poor cat was as thin as a rake.

"Well – I thought at least you could be trusted to feed my cat!" said his friend Pippy, almost in tears. "Poor, poor Whiskers – I'd never have gone away and left him if I'd thought you wouldn't feed him."

"So sorry!" said Rilloby, and he really did feel very sorry about it. But all the same, when Dame Ricky asked him to feed her hens and give them water

while she was in bed with a bad leg he forgot after the first day – and the hens became very thin and didn't lay any more eggs.

"That fellow simply can't be trusted!" said Dame Ricky. "He's always so ready to promise anything – and then he doesn't do it. I'd rather be like old Mr Mean – not promise anything! At least you know where you are with him."

At last everyone got so annoyed with Rilloby that they decided to do something about it. Why should they put up with him when he behaved like that? He deserved a jolly good lesson!

"And we'll give it to him!" said Dame Ricky, who felt very angry about her hens. "Now – let's all think hard and

35

see what we can do to show Rilloby what he's really like."

"I've got an idea!" said Pippy, Rilloby's neighbour. "It's his birthday, soon, isn't it?"

"Yes – in two weeks' time," said Mister Doodle. "What's your idea, Pippy?"

"Well – shall we all get very excited about it and plan a big party for him and lots of presents – and let him know all about it? And then shall we do as he does – not bother – forget – and make him see how horrid it is when something is promised and not done?" said Pippy.

"It seems rather unkind," said Dame Get-Along. "But, on the other hand, it may be kind in the end, if it teaches him how horrid it is to be untrustworthy. A trustworthy person is such a good friend to have. Rilloby is no good at all. He makes other people suffer so much through his carelessness."

"My poor cat almost died through

him," said Pippy. "I think it's time Rilloby had a taste of his own medicine."

Well, that was all settled then. Rilloby was to see what it felt like when people planned things and promised them and then didn't remember or didn't bother!

Rilloby was very pleased indeed when everyone began to talk about his birthday. It sounded to him as if he was going to have a very good time!

"I'll make you a fine cake, Rilloby," said Dame Get-Along. "Let me see now – have I got any sugar roses? Yes, I have.

And plenty of candles to put on it, too. Yes, I'll see if I can make you a really grand cake!"

"Oh, thank you!" said Rilloby, beaming.

"And I'll get my friend Jinky, the conjurer, along," said Mr Doodle. "He's a wonderful fellow for a party. You should see the things he does! Why, at the last party he poured six bottles of lemonade out of a small teapot! Think of that!"

"Oooh – I'd love all that lemonade!" said Rilloby. "There would be enough for everyone!"

"I'll try and make you a musical box," said Pippy, who was very clever at that kind of thing. "One that will play all sorts of dance tunes for you!"

"Oh, *thank* you!" said Rilloby. "We could dance at my party then. That would be lovely!"

"I'll bake you some biscuits and buns, and make some of my special ice-cream," said Dame Ricky. Rilloby beamed. What a lovely time he was going to have!

Other people promised all kinds of things, too. "I will send you along a new suit to wear at the party," said Mrs Thimble. "I've a bit of red and gold stuff that would suit you very well, Rilloby."

"A party suit!" cried Rilloby, looking down at his rather dirty old suit. "Just what I want!"

"And if I've time I'll go along to the Long-Tail Bird and ask him for one of his fallen feathers for your hat," said Trotty. "It's nice to have a fine, long feather in a hat."

Well, Rilloby was quite overjoyed to hear of all these wonderful things. He sat down at once and wrote out invitations to his birthday party. He

39

sent the cards to this three brothers, his two sisters, his six aunts, his five uncles, and his seven cousins.

"Do come!" he wrote. "There will be biscuits and buns and a fine, big birthday cake with sugar roses and candles. There will be ice-cream to eat and a new musical box to dance to. We shall have a wonderful conjurer to do tricks for us. I am having a red and gold suit and a feather in my hat!"

Everyone accepted, of course. They thought it sounded a most wonderful party. Rilloby was beside himself with joy. What a lot of good friends he had! Fancy their promising him so many things!

His birthday came. He had plenty of

40

cards, of course. He rubbed his hands in glee when he thought of the afternoon. He wondered when Mrs Thimble would send him along his party suit. He was longing to try it on.

At half-past three Rilloby felt worried. The party was to begin at four. But Mrs Thimble hadn't brought his suit and Trotty hadn't been along with the feather to put in his hat.

Rilloby was dressed in his dirty old suit, for he hadn't bothered to wash, brush or mend it because he meant to wear the new one that Mrs Thimble had promised him. At five to four he was very worried indeed.

41

"I shall have no time to change in to my new suit when Mrs Thimble brings it!" he groaned. "Oh dear, oh dear! Here come my first guests!"

They were his sisters and brothers. They looked surprised to see Rilloby so dirty and untidy.

"My party suit hasn't arrived yet," he explained. "It will come soon. Ah – here is Mrs Thimble. I expect she's got it with her."

But she hadn't! When Rilloby asked her about it, she looked quite puzzled. Then she said, "Oh yes – I believe I did promise you one. But I forgot all about it, Rilloby. Anyway, you forgot to deliver a whole lot of parcels for me once, do you remember? So that makes us even, doesn't it? I forgave you, and you must forgive me!"

Poor Rilloby! He knew then that he would have to wear his dirty old suit, and how ashamed he felt! But there was no help for it. At least his *hat* would look smart when Trotty brought along the feather!

But Trotty didn't bring it. "Oh, sorry, old man," he said to Rilloby. "I couldn't be bothered to go along to the Long-Tail Bird. He lives so far away. So sorry."

And then Pippy came along – but he brought no beautiful musical box with him! "Did I say I'd make you one? Oh yes, I did!" he said. "Well, I've been awfully busy, Rilloby. So sorry. I know you'll forgive me, because do you remember how you forgot to feed my cat when I was away – so that makes us even, doesn't it? We've both been forgetful!"

Rilloby went red. Then he saw Dame Ricky bustling in. "Ah – she said she'd bring me biscuits, buns and ice-cream!" thought Rilloby and ran to meet her. But her hands were empty!

"I didn't have time to go and get the flour and sugar from the grocer for the biscuits," she said. "So sorry, Rilloby. And I'm afraid I forgot all about the ice-cream! Still, you're so forgetful yourself that you'll understand that. You remember, don't you, how you forgot to feed my hens for me? Well, I'm as sorry about forgetting the ice-cream as you were about my hens."

Then Mr Doodle came – and he hadn't brought his friend Jinky, the conjurer! "It was rather a bother to find his address," he told Rilloby. "I do hope you won't mind my not bringing him. I expect you remember that it was too much trouble for you to fetch the plumber for me once – so you'll forgive me for not bringing Jinky!"

And then Dame Get-Along arrived – without any birthday cake! Rilloby almost burst into tears.

"I'm *so* sorry, Rilloby!" said Dame Get-Along. "Did I really say I'd make you a cake? I'm getting forgetful in my old age! But there, you're so forgetful yourself that you won't mind, I'm sure!"

But Rilloby did mind. He minded dreadfully. It was his birthday, and this was his party – and here he was in a dirty old suit, with no feather in his

45

hat, no buns, biscuits or cake or ice-cream to eat, no conjurer or musical box, nothing at all! And all his brothers and sisters, aunts, uncles and cousins to feed and entertain!

His oldest aunt, Aunt Jerusha, was very angry indeed. "A party without anything to eat! And you in a dirty, torn suit, Rilloby! You should be ashamed of yourself. I'm going home!"

Well, everyone went home, of course, and Rilloby was left alone. He sat in a corner and cried. He sobbed very bitterly indeed. "I see what they did!" he wept. "They did it to punish me! I

forget things so often, I don't bother myself about other people as I should, I'm careless and thoughtless. And now they've shown me what it feels like when people behave as I do."

Tears ran down his cheeks and dripped on to his shoes. "I thought they liked me and they don't. They're all laughing at me, and they're glad they've made me miserable on my birthday!"

"Oh no we aren't," said a voice, and Pippy put his head in at the window. "We're sorry for you. But we knew we'd have to teach you a lesson. Have you learnt it, Rilloby?"

"Of course! I'll never, never forget today," sobbed Rilloby.

"Well – come along into my house, then," said Pippy, smiling. "We've got a small birthday cake for you, and some buns and a little ice-cream. And just a few tiny presents! You'll find in my house all the people who taught you this horrid lesson – so if you like to come along and tell them what you've just told me, we'll have a little birthday party after all!"

Rilloby dried his eyes. He cheered up. He went with Pippy to his house and saw Dame Get-Along there and all the rest. And, because he was a sensible fellow after all, he told them that he *had* learnt his lesson and was glad of it. Then they all sat down and had a very nice little party indeed. Rilloby turned over a new leaf after that, as you can guess – but his Aunt Jerusha never spoke to him again!

The Little Carol Singer

"What's the matter with John?" said Grandfather in surprise. "He does look miserable!"

"Well, he's got a cold, and so he can't go out carol-singing with the school choir," said John's mother. "He's upset because he does so love carols – and he's got a lovely voice, you know."

"Yes, I know," said Grandfather. "So had I when I was a boy like John. Tell John to come along to me. I've got something to tell him."

John came, and went over to his grandfather. The old man put his arm round him and smiled. "So you are disappointed because you can't go carol-singing. What carols were you going to sing?"

"Oh – lovely ones: 'Good King Wenceslas', and 'Nowell, Nowell', and 'The Holy Babe' – and 'Here We Come A'wassailing'. I love that one," said John. "I don't know what 'wassailing' means, though."

"It means a merry party, where wassail was drunk," said his grandfather. "It's a very old carol, you know. I used to sing it as a boy too. I remember one time very well indeed."

"Tell me about it, Grandfather," said John. He liked to hear the old man's stories of his long-ago boyhood.

"Well," said Grandfather, "I was about six years old, I suppose, and it was wintertime, very cold and frosty. There were my mother and I and my little sister Hannah, all living in a tiny cottage together."

"Where was your father?" asked John.

"He was dead," said Grandfather. "He left my mother a little money but it soon went – and that winter, when Christmas was near, my poor mother

50

couldn't even pay the rent of the little cottage."

"What happened?" asked John. "Was she turned out?"

"The landlord was a hard man," said his grandfather. "He said that unless she could find some money to give him, she must be turned out of her cottage with my little sister and I. We had nowhere to go, and it was bitter weather. I remember my mother crying bitterly."

"What did you do?" asked John.

"Well, I made up my mind that *I* must get some money somehow," said Grandfather. "So I put on my cap and coat and out I went into the snow. But nobody wanted a little boy's work!

Nobody wanted snow swept away, or errands run. I didn't get a single penny."

"Poor Grandfather," said John. "I would have given you everything in my moneybox. Yes, even my bright new pound coin!"

"I began to trudge home in the snow, cold and hungry," went on the old man. "I even remember how numb my hands were and how I put them under my armpits to try and warm them. And then, as it grew dark, I heard the sound of singing."

"What was it? Carol-singers?" asked John.

"Yes. It was a party of villagers, going from house to house, singing all kinds of carols," said Grandfather. "In those days the big houses threw open their doors to the singers, and welcomed them in, and gave them mulled wine and spiced apples, and little cakes."

"That sounds nice," said John. "I should like a spiced apple. What did you do next, Grandfather? Please tell me."

"I thought of the spiced apples and little cakes," said Grandfather. "And I was so hungry that I felt I really must have something to eat. So I joined the party of carol-singers, without being seen, and went with them up the long drive to the Squire's house."

"Were you found out?" asked John.

"I sang with them," said Grandfather, remembering that long ago evening clearly. "We sang 'The Holy Babe'. I remember then the door opened, and the Squire himself welcomed us in. I went in too, scared but so cold and hungry that I longed to see a fire, and have something to eat."

"Was there a nice fire?" said John.

"An enormous one," went on Grandfather. "It was blazing up in the big hall. The Squire's lady was there, pretty and kind and smiling – and on a big table there were jugs of warm drinks, and dishes of spiced apples and plates of little cakes. I could hardly take my eyes off them. But before we could eat and drink, we had to sing again."

"What did you sing?" asked John.

"The carol you said you liked," said his grandfather. "'Here We Come A-wassailing'. I sang too, because I knew the words and the tune. And I remember the villagers turning to stare

at me and wondering how I came to be with them. I remember the Squire's lady looking at me, and listening to my voice. And at the end she said, "Little boy, you have a very sweet voice. I would like to hear you sing by yourself."

"Oh Grandfather – what happened then?" asked John.

"I sang the chorus of 'Here We Come A-wassailing," said Grandfather, "and everyone listened, because in those days I had a lovely voice. And then the Squire's lady gave me something hot to drink, and a spiced apple and two little cakes. I drank my drink and ate the spiced apple – but I put the cakes into my pocket."

"Why? To take home?" asked John.

"Yes. For my mother and sister," said Grandfather. "But one of the villagers saw me stuffing the cakes into my pocket and he was angry. I think he thought I had taken them from the table when nobody was looking. He began to scold me – and what with the hot drink, and the blazing fire, and the thought of going home to my mother without anything at all to give her, I suddenly found tears pouring down my cheeks. I was so ashamed. I tried to stumble to the door and go."

"Did they let you?" asked John. "Poor Grandfather! What a horrid ending to your evening!"

"Oh, that wasn't the end," said Grandfather. "The Squire's lady jumped up, put her arms round me and led me to a seat by the fire. 'Now you tell me why you are sad,' she said. 'A boy with a voice like yours shouldn't be sad! He should be glad!'"

"She was nice," said John.

"So I told her everything," said Grandfather. "About my mother and

sister, and how we had no money and how the next day we were all to be turned out in the snow. I told her I had no right to be with the carol-singers, or to eat her apples and cakes. But by that time the others had gone on their way and I was left with the Squire and his lady."

"Go on, Grandfather," begged John. "This is a much nicer ending! It is all true, isn't it?"

"Oh yes!" said Grandfather. "Quite true. The Squire took me home to my mother, and told her that he had a fine little cottage she could go to the next day, and pay no rent for – but he wanted one thing in return."

"What was it?" asked John.

"He wanted my mother to let me learn singing and music, and to have my voice trained – and he said that when I grew up and earned money by my voice and music, then I could pay him back," said Grandfather. "My mother could hardly believe her ears!"

"Oh, Grandfather – and that was how you became such a famous singer and musician!" cried John. "All because you went carolling one night, hungry and cold!"

"Yes. So now you know why, like you, I love the old carol, 'Here We Come A-wassailing'," said Grandfather. "Let's call Mother and go to the piano and sing it together, shall we? And I shall remember again the time when I too went 'wassailing' years and years ago!"

Jiffy
Gets Into Trouble

When Little Sing-Song came up the lane throwing her new ball into the air Jiffy hid behind a hedge in his garden and watched her.

Sing-Song was singing as usual as she threw her ball up and caught it.

"Up you go,
Ever so high.
If I'm not careful
You'll touch the sky!"

And at the last line little Sing-Song sent the ball up very high indeed. She hardly ever caught it when she threw it so high, and then it bounced and she had to run after it, laughing.

"Down you go
And you bounce away.
'You can't catch me!'
I can hear you say!"

Jiffy watched for Sing-Song to throw up her ball again. She was near his hedge. Suppose she missed it and it bounced into his garden – he could get it before she did and keep it. She wouldn't know!

Up went the ball again, and Sing-Song began her funny little song once more.

"Up you go,
Ever so high.
If I'm not careful
You'll touch the sky!"

And at the last line she sent the ball so high into the air that for one moment Jiffy thought it *might* touch the sky. But it didn't, of course. It began to fall, and, to Jiffy's delight, it came over his garden. He reached out

his hands and caught it!

Sing-Song didn't see him, because he was behind the bush. She opened the gate and ran in.

"Mrs Jiffy, Mrs Jiffy!" she called. "Can I come in and get my ball?"

"Of course!" called Jiffy's mother from the cottage. "Come in, little Sing-Song."

But when Sing-Song came in she couldn't find the ball anywhere. That wasn't surprising, because Jiffy had hidden it under the bush. He came out grinning.

His mother saw him. "Jiffy! Now, Jiffy, *you* haven't got Sing-Song's ball, have you? Because if you have you must give it to her. Don't be naughty, now."

"I haven't got it," said Jiffy.

But still his mother wasn't certain. She knew Jiffy wasn't always truthful, and it made her sad. She looked at him sharply.

"Well, you look hard for it," she said. "And I'll come and look, too!"

Jiffy was alarmed. He didn't want his mother to come and look for the ball. She would be certain to find it under the bush – and she would guess he had hidden it there. So he told a story.

"I know where it is," he said. "I saw it fall. It fell on our roof and rolled into the gutter that goes round it to catch the rain."

"Well, you go and borrow Mr Tinky's big, long stick," said his mother. "You can easily reach the ball with that. Can you wait till he borrows the stick, Sing-Song?"

"No, I'm afraid I can't," said Sing-Song. "My mother is waiting for me to catch the bus with her. But perhaps Jiffy could leave the ball at our house if he gets it out of the gutter for me? Goodbye!"

She skipped off, singing one of her little songs.

"My ball is lost,
Oh, what a pity!
It really was
So very pretty!"

"Funny little singing thing," said Mrs Jiffy, smiling after Sing-Song. "Jiffy, what are you standing there like that for? Didn't you hear me tell you to go and borrow Mr Tinky's big stick?"

Now Mr Tinky lived a long way away, and Jiffy didn't want to go and borrow a stick to poke at a gutter for a ball that wasn't there. But he couldn't tell his mother that. So he pretended to go. He went out of the front gate and then crept in again at the back and sat in the shed reading. When he thought it was about time for him to say he was back from Mr Tinky's he put down his book and strolled into the house.

"Oh – so there you are," said his mother. "Where is Mr Tinky's stick?"

Jiffy made up a story at once. He was clever at that! "Oh, Ma, Mr Tinky's sorry, but he had burglars last night, and he broke his stick chasing them away."

"Well, I never! Burglars! And how brave of old Mr Tinky to chase them away!" said his mother. "Dear me! Well, Jiffy, you must go along to Mrs Gobbo and ask her to lend you her step-ladder. She's got a nice big one. Mine's too small."

"Blow!" said Jiffy to himself. He wanted to read his book. He didn't want to borrow a step-ladder to find a ball that was still safely under the bush! So he did exactly the same thing again – walked out of the front gate and crept in again at the back.

In twenty minutes' time he came out of the shed! "Ma! Mrs Gobbo's sorry, but she says – er – she says that poor Mr Gobbo climbed up on the step-ladder yesterday and it broke and he

64

fell off and hurt his back. So she can't lend it to anyone until it's mended."

"Good gracious me! I do hope poor old Gobbo isn't badly hurt," said Mrs Jiffy in surprise. "What a sad thing! Well, Jiffy, you must go to Mr Tock now and ask him for that ladder of his. It's far too long, of course, but that won't matter. It will be rather heavy for you to carry, but you're a strong boy. Go along and get the ladder."

This was too bad! "First it's a stick; then it's a step-ladder, now it's a ladder!" groaned Jiffy to himself. "Why ever did I tell that story about Sing-Song's ball being in the gutter? It's made me tell bigger and bigger stories all the morning. Well – I suppose I'd better pretend to get Mr Tock's ladder! But I only hope this is the last thing Ma wants me to fetch!"

He went out of the front gate and crept in at the back for the third time. He took up his book again. He was quite lost in it, and read for a long time. Then he heard his mother calling.

"Jiffy! Jiffy! Aren't you back from Mr Tock's yet? Where's the ladder?"

Jiffy ran out of the shed in a hurry, trying to think of something to tell his mother.

"Oh, Ma, yes – here I am. But I couldn't borrow his ladder. He's painting his house, and he's using it."

"Painting his house! Why, he only painted it last week, from top to bottom!" said Mrs Jiffy, amazed. "Why in the world is he doing it again?"

"Er – well," said Jiffy, thinking hard, "somebody horrid came by his house in the night and splashed red and blue paint all over it. It was such a sight that Mr Tock is going to paint it all again."

"Poor Mr Tock!" said his mother. "Well, well, well – the things that do happen! I would send you for Dame Goose's ladder, Jiffy, If only it wasn't dinnertime. I do wish we could get Sing-Song's ball for her somehow."

Jiffy was beginning to get very tired of Sing-Song's ball. It was still under

the bush. He hoped his mother would forget all about it that afternoon because she was going to a party. Then he could play with the ball and see how high he could throw it and how well it bounced. It certainly was the very finest ball he had ever seen!

Mrs Jiffy did seem to forget about the ball after dinner. She went to get herself ready for the party. Jiffy wasn't going. He was to stay and look after the house and feed the hens and ducks.

Off went Mrs Jiffy at three o'clock, looking very nice in her new hat. She walked down the lane, and very soon met Mr Tinky. Jiffy had said that the old man had broken his stick chasing burglars away – but here he was, with his stick, tapping along as usual!

"I suppose he's got it mended already," said Mrs Jiffy to herself. "Good afternoon, Mr Tinky. I'm so sorry you had the burglars last night. I hope they didn't take anything."

"Burglars? What burglars?" said old Mr Tinky thinking he couldn't have heard properly. "*I* didn't know I had burglars. Nobody told me."

"But, Mr Tinky – you chased them – you were very brave," said Mrs Jiffy. "You broke your stick on them!"

"I didn't," said Mr Tinky. "Here's my stick – and it's not broken, is it? Who told you all that nonsense?"

Mrs Jiffy didn't answer. How very extraordinary! Jiffy had certainly told her about the burglars. She was thinking hard about this when she arrived at Mrs Doddle's, where the party was to be held. And going in at the gate, whom did she see but Mr and Mrs Gobbo!

She stared at Mr Gobbo! Well, well – Jiffy had told her that the poor old fellow had fallen off the step-ladder and hurt his back. She was glad it was better so soon.

"Well, Mr Gobbo! How's your poor back?" she said kindly. Mr Gobbo stared in surprise.

"It's all right. Nothing wrong with it as far as I know," he said.

"But – you fell off the step-ladder when it broke," said Mrs Jiffy.

"What step-ladder? Ours isn't broken," said Mrs Gobbo. "Someone's been telling you a tale, Mrs Jiffy! Mr Gobbo is right as rain, and so is our step-ladder!"

Mrs Jiffy began to feel cross. Jiffy had *certainly* told her all about Mr Gobbo. How could he have known about it if Mrs Gobbo hadn't told him? It was very strange. And then she saw Mr Tock, who was also a guest at the party. She hurried to him.

"Mr Tock! How tiresome of someone to splash red and blue paint all over

70

your newly painted house! I was so sorry you had to paint it all over again."

Mr Tock stared at Mrs Jiffy as if she had gone mad.

"Madam," he said, "no one has splashed red and blue paint over my house as far as I know. And as for painting it all over again, I shouldn't dream of it. What are you talking about?"

"But, Mr Tock, don't you remember – you used your long ladder to paint your house outside this very morning!" cried Mrs Jiffy. "Jiffy went to borrow it, and you said he couldn't because you were using it."

Mr Tock pricked up his ears. So did Mr and Mrs Gobbo and Mr Tinky. "Oho

71

– it was *Jiffy* who told you that, was it?" said Mr Tock. "Well, we know Jiffy and his great big stories. He's just been telling you fibs, as usual, Mrs Jiffy – didn't want to do something, I suppose, so he made up all kinds of fairy-tales."

"He didn't come to borrow our step-ladder," said Mrs Gobbo.

"And he didn't come to borrow my stick," said Mr Tinky. "But I'll lend it to him, Mrs Jiffy. I'll certainly lend it to him. You send him along to me this evening, and I'll lend it to him all right!"

"Ah, yes – you do that," said Mrs Gobbo.

"I think I *will* send him," said poor Mrs Jiffy, looking very sad. "He's a naughty boy. He'll have to be stopped or goodness knows what will happen to him. I'll send him along this evening, Mr Tinky – and you can lend him your stick. Lend it to him hard, won't you?"

And, to Jiffy's great astonishment, when his mother got home after tea she told him he was to go straight off to

Mr Tinky's and borrow his stick.

"It's mended now," said his mother, looking straight at him. "Quite mended. And the burglars have all gone. He can use his stick for other bad people again. You go along and ask him to lend it to you."

"Oh, Ma – don't make me!" cried Jiffy in a fright. He didn't like the look on his mother's face at all. "I'll get you the ball – I hid it under the bush. It didn't go in the gutter – and that's why I didn't go and borrow sticks and ladders to get it down. That would have been silly."

"It would," said his mother. "Very silly. I've felt very silly this afternoon, too, saying I was sorry about burglars and bad backs, and repainted houses. But now Mr Tinky *wants* to lend you his stick, so you must go. I'll get the ball, and when you get back you can take it to Sing-Song and say you're sorry. Go along."

Well, there was nothing for it but to go. Jiffy doesn't want to. He doesn't like Mr Tinky's stick, and he's going to like it even less now. Hurry up, Jiffy, and go. It's your own fault, you know, and I don't feel sorry for you one bit!

The Boy Who Never Put Things Back

Did you ever know a boy called George, who could never remember to put things back into their places? Well, this is a story about him.

George was about ten years old, and he had two brothers and two sisters, all older than he was. They were fond of George, although they often called him the baby of the family, which he didn't like at all. He was always trying to be big and grown-up, so that his brothers and sisters would take him about with them and let him join in their games.

"I don't like being left out of things just because I'm the youngest," he said to his mother. "It's not fair. I can't help being the youngest."

"There's no need for you to be left

out," his mother said. "Behave yourself, be kind to the others, do odd jobs for them when you can, and you will see they will take you out on picnics with them."

There was one thing that George was always getting into trouble for – and that was, he never would put things back into their places! Do you know anyone like that? They are really most annoying people.

George used to like cutting out from papers and magazines, but he had no scissors of his own. So what did he do but go to his big sister Mary's work basket and borrow her scissors. But when he had finished cutting out, he wouldn't put the scissors back again! No, he would leave them on the table, and then someone would clear them away.

When Mary wanted them, they wouldn't be in her work basket, and then she would spend half an hour hunting for them. That would make her very cross.

"I don't mind you borrowing my things, but you might at least have the decency to put them back!" she would say to George.

Then he would borrow Alec's pencil and leave it lying somewhere in the garden. Or he would go off with Mother's pen to write a letter and not take it back. She would find it in his pocket a week later, when she had given up looking for it.

His mother and all his older brothers and sisters scolded him well for this silly habit, but although George kept promising to be better, he wasn't. He was too lazy-minded to try and remember to take borrowed things back.

Now one summer everyone was in a great state of excitement because they were going to the seaside. The older children were going to ride down on their bicycles, picnic on the way, spend a night at a camp, and then join the rest of the family at the hotel next day.

George listened to all the arrangements being made. When he heard that only the four older ones were to ride down to the sea and he was to go by train the next day, he was angry and hurt.

"Mother! Why can't *I* go with the others? I'm ten, aren't I? Why can't I ride with them? I've got a lovely new bicycle, I'm a very good rider, and I want to go with the others."

"Don't talk like that to me, George," said his mother. "That's not the way to get anything you want. You wouldn't be able to ride so far."

"Oh, Mother, I could, I could!" said George, and he put his arms round his mother to coax her. "Let me, please. Ask Alec if I can't ride well now! Ask Mary! I went all the way to the woods and back with her last week. Oh, do, do let me. I can't tell you how much I want to ride off with the others, and sleep in a camp for the night. I don't want to be a baby and go by train."

"I should think you could let him come with us, Mother," said Alec. "He's good on his bike. I'll look after him. It would be nice for him to have his bike by the sea too, because then he could come for rides and picnics with us. Otherwise he won't be able to."

They all talked it over, and to George's enormous delight Mother at last decided to let him ride off with the others. How simply marvellous!

"I shall feel so big," thought George,

as he polished up his bicycle the next day. "Fancy going off all by ourselves – and sleeping in a camp for the night!"

The bicycles were kept in two sheds. Alec's, Mary's, Peter's and Jane's went in one shed, and George's, his mother's and his father's went in the other. They were all good bicycles, and their father insisted that they should be well looked after and cleaned each week.

The children thought the day would never come for them to start off. But at last the day before came, and they all took out their bicycles for a last polish and to make sure they had no punctures. They put them back into

the sheds, shut the doors and went to help their mother with the last-minute packing.

George was having a friend to tea. It was Penny, the little girl from next door. She collected stamps and so did George. They had five stamp albums each, and they went to tea with one another once a week to swap stamps, stick them into their albums and gloat over their collections.

After tea the two of them took out their stamp albums. Penny bent over hers – and then she sat up with a cry. A spot of red had fallen on to her precious album!

"Oh, George – my nose is bleeding

81

again! I shall have to sit with my head back till it stops. Wipe that spot carefully off the page for me."

"Bother!" said George, looking at Penny. Her nose often bled and it was such a nuisance because then she had to stop whatever she was doing.

"Mother's busy," said George, "or I'd fetch her."

"It's all right," said Penny, mopping her nose. "It'll soon stop. It never lasts long."

But it did seem to last a long time. Penny lay down on her back on the floor to try and stop it. But it still didn't.

"We're wasting all this time," said George. "Is there anything else to do for nose-bleeding besides lying on the floor?"

"Well, once Granny put the biggest key she had down my back," said Penny. "She said that would stop it."

"What a funny idea!" said George. "Shall we try it? I know where there is a very big key."

"All right. Fetch it," said poor Penny.

"You can stick it down my back and perhaps the coldness will stop the bleeding."

George sped off to the bicycle shed where his bike was kept. There was a very big key in the lock there. He took it out and ran back. He pushed it down Penny's back. She squealed.

"Oooh! It's terribly cold. Oooh, it makes me wriggle!"

But very soon the nose-bleeding stopped and she could sit up. "I don't know if it was the key or whether it was really going to stop," she said. "Anyway, I'm better now. Let's get on with our stamps."

So they got on with their stamps and had a fine time swapping and arranging. Then it was time for Penny to go.

"Goodbye," she said. "Come to tea with me as soon as you get back. I hope you have a fine holiday."

"I'm biking down with the others!" said George grandly. "Going to spend a night at a camp! It'll be fine."

The next day came. The children were to set off at ten o'clock. They had their few night things with them in kitbags, and their packages of food. Mother gave George his, too. He did feel proud.

"Now get your bikes, and I'll come to the front gate to see you off," she said. "Take care of George, Peter."

They all went to get their bikes. Alec, Mary, Peter and Jane wheeled theirs out of the shed. But George couldn't get his.

"The other shed's locked," he said. "I can't get my bike."

"Well, unlock it, silly!" called Alec. "Can't you turn the key?"

"It's not here," said George, and he rattled the door.

Mother came up. "What's the matter? Don't shake the door like that."

"Mother, the key's gone. I can't get my bike," said George in a panic.

"Well, where *is* the key?" said Mother. "It can't be far away. Has anyone taken it?"

"Oh!" said George, remembering suddenly. "Yes, I took it! Penny's nose bled yesterday, and I borrowed the key to put down her back. It must be in the playroom." He sped off to get it. He hunted everywhere for it. It didn't seem to be anywhere at all. Alec yelled up to him.

"Oh, do come on, George. It's quarter-past ten. We shall never get to camp tonight if we start late now."

"Oh, wait for me, wait for me!" cried poor George, tearing about the room and hunting for the key. Mother came up and helped him.

"George, I don't know how many times I've told you to put things back when you've borrowed them," she said. "Now you see what's happened! You're making everybody late."

"Let's try the key of the other shed," said Mary. So they did, but it didn't fit.

"Well, we can't wait any more," said Peter at half-past ten. "We must go. George must come with you by train, Mother."

"Oh no, oh no! Wait for me! Don't go without me!" begged George. "Oh, I couldn't bear it. Mother, can't we break open the door to get my bike?"

"Certainly not," said Mother. "Now, George, this is entirely your own fault. You will have to put up with the results of your silliness. You took the key and you should have put it back. You didn't, so we can't get your bike. The others are not going to wait, so you will have to go with us tomorrow."

And that is just what happened. The others mounted their bicycles, waved goodbye and set off – without poor George. He was ten, and a big boy, but he was so bitterly disappointed that he went to the bottom of the garden and cried by himself for a whole hour.

Daddy was not very comforting that night when he heard about it. "Well, sooner or later I knew that silly habit of yours of taking things and never putting them back would bring you a good punishment," he said. "It's a pity, George – but if you do things like that you must expect things to go wrong."

"I wish I knew where the key was!" said George. "Oh, Mother – if I don't find it I suppose I can't take my bike away on the train?"

"You certainly can't," said Mother. So George spent the whole evening hunting for that key, but he couldn't find it. He had to go to bed very sad indeed.

The next day Mother, Daddy and George got ready for the train. Just about ten minutes before the taxi-cab came, Penny came running up.

"George! Did you want the key you put down my back yesterday? I went home with it still down my back, but I thought I had better bring it to you this morning in case it was important."

"Oh, Penny! You horrid, horrid girl! You went off with the key! Now I haven't been able to go with the others," said George, and he almost slapped Penny.

"Stop that, George!" said his father at once. "It was you who should have thought of the key and taken it back, not Penny. I won't have you blaming anyone else. That's a coward's trick. Take the blame yourself, as you should, and act properly."

"Sorry, Penny," said George, feeling really ashamed. His father nodded to his mother.

"Well, as George seems to be sorry, he can take his bike with him. There's just time to get it before the taxi comes. He can bring it on the train with him."

George sped off with the key. He got out his bike. Now at least he would be able to go for rides with the others. But oh, what a pity he hadn't been able to go with them the day before! That would have been such a wonderful treat!

"I shall always put things back in future," thought George. "I gave myself a terrible disappointment by forgetting about the key. I won't let things like this happen again."

Did you guess where the key was? You are clever if you did!

The
Proud Fir Tree

There was once a beautiful fir tree that lived in a wood. It was the only fir tree there, and it thought a good deal of itself.

The other trees around it were oak and beech and hazel, and they were none of them quite so tall as the fir.

Once some children had come into the wood and had seen the fir.

"Look!" said the boy. "See that fir? Hasn't it got a lovely straight trunk! Did you know that the masts of ships were made from fir tree trunks, Rosie?"

"Are they really?" said Rosie, looking up the straight trunk of the fir.

"Yes – and telegraph poles too," said the boy. "Not many trees grow such fine straight trunks, Rosie."

Well, the fir tree was tremendously proud to hear all this. It swayed about in the wind, and made a little song up about itself:

"Telegraph poles are made from me,
And the masts of ships that sail on
the sea!"

The other trees got tired of this song. "After all, a good many things are made from us, too," said the oak. "I make lots of beautiful furniture – and the beams in the roofs of many famous old buildings are made of oak."

"And I am used for heaps of things too," said the graceful beech.

"The gamekeeper comes and cuts his walking-sticks from my branches," said the hazel.

And even the little willow by the stream had something to say too. "I help to make cricket bats," it said.

When the autumn came, the beeches and the oaks and all the other trees in the wood flamed into brilliant colour. You should have seen them! The beech was a mass of gold.

The fir was quite jealous of them then. "I suppose you think you are lovely, turning strange colours all of a sudden," it said.

"Well, the children think we are lovely," said the beech. "They like to pick up some of my golden leaves and take them to school. And they pluck some of my sprays and press them so that they may have vases full of my golden leaves in the winter."

"Let me tell you this," said the fir. "Every autumn you dress yourselves proudly in gold, red, brown, and yellow. And then what happens to you? The

93

frost comes along and loosens all your leaves – and the wind sweeps them off the boughs. Your fine dresses lie scattered on the muddy ground – and you are left bare and cold all through the winter days!"

"That is quite true," said the oak.

"And what about me?" said the fir. "It is true that I don't dress myself up in yellows and reds – but I am sensible enough to keep my branches green all the winter long! I don't stand cold and bare and ugly."

The other trees knew that this was true. They waved their bare boughs in the wind, whilst the fir waved her green-clad branches in pride.

"Are we really ugly now?" said the oak sadly. "I wonder why we shed our pretty leaves? It does seem rather a waste to have to grow them every year."

"Perhaps the fir is more sensible than we are, after all," said the hazel.

"Telegraph poles are made from me,
And the masts of ships that sail on
   the sea!"

sang the fir tree.

Now that winter the sky suddenly became a strange grey leaden colour. The trees looked up, half afraid.

"Why is the sky so low and grey?" said the oak. "I don't like it. And listen – the wind is getting up!"

A cold wind blew. The bare trees waved their branches and the fir tree shouted in the wind.

Then snow fell. It fell steadily all the night long. It didn't stop once. The sky was full of snow. When the morning came, the wood looked so different. It was quite white!

"What a snowstorm!" said the oak, shaking its sturdy boughs. The snow fell off at once.

But the oak's branches were soon white with snow again, for there was still plenty of snow to come. All day long it fell, and on the hills it was more than a metre deep.

Then the fir tree began to grumble loudly. "Oh, this snow! Oh, this heavy, heavy snow! I can't bear the weight of it any longer!"

"Well, shake it off then, as we do," said the oak.

"How can I!" said the fir tree crossly. "You have bare branches, so that the snow cannot cling to you as it can to

96

my green branches! I hold the snow with all my boughs. Oh, how heavy it is! Stop snowing, sky! I can bear the weight no longer!"

But the snow went on snowing. Then there came a loud CRACK! All the trees were startled. What could it be? They could see nothing.

"I'm afraid I am breaking," said the fir tree sadly. "That was one of my branches."

CRACK! Another branch broke. The fir tree shivered. A mass of snow slipped down from its branches.

CRACK!

"Good gracious! The fir tree will be broken to bits!" said the oak. "I do hope the snow soon stops."

It stopped very soon. Then the weather turned warmer and all the snow melted. The trees stretched themselves and looked at the fir tree.

Poor, poor thing! All its beautiful branches were broken and hung sadly down. One was already on the ground. It was no longer beautiful.

"Why did I boast that I kept my leaves?" said the fir tree sadly. "If I had thrown them down as you did, Oak tree, the snow would have slipped easily from my boughs, and they would not have broken beneath the great weight of the snow. Oh, what an unhappy tree I am! I am ashamed of my looks now. I shall never, never sing my little song again."

"We will grow our branches more closely around you to hide your broken sides," promised the beech. "After all, you still have a fine straight trunk."

So the other trees grew their branches quite close to the fir, and hid the places where his dead branches had fallen off. He was grateful and friendly.

"Well, Fir tree, you may not be so beautiful now, but you are much nicer to know!" said the oak next summer, when his leaves whispered by the thousand.

"That's something!" said the fir tree, stretching his high head to the sky. "That's certainly something."

On
Firework Night

Jinky the gnome came rushing down the village street, shouting at the top of his voice. "The green goblin has got Pippy and Tickles and Hoho! He's caught them and taken them to his castle!"

Everyone came running out to hear the bad news. "That goblin! We've had nothing but bad luck ever since he came to our village," said Dame Shuffle.

"However are we to rescue Pippy and the others?" asked Old Man Spectacles. "He'll shut them up in his castle and keep them prisoners for always. He'll never let them out, never!"

"We're none of us safe nowadays," said Mother Bonnet. "That goblin! I'd like to have him here this very minute. I'd give him such a whacking with my stick."

"You wouldn't. You'd run to your cottage, shut the door, and bolt it," said Dame Shuffle. "We're all scared of him, and that's the truth."

"Yes, we are," said Jinky. "But scared or not, somehow we've got to rescue our friends."

But that wasn't going to be easy! The green goblin locked them up in his castle on the hill outside the village, and wouldn't let them out at all. They had to help him with his spells, cook his

101

meals, sweep his floors and make his bed. How they hated it!

A little mouse lived in a hole behind the kitchen wall. Pip asked him to take a note to Jinky for him. The mouse disappeared with it, and faithfully delivered it to Jinky.

Jinky read the note. "Please, please think of some way to save us. We can't even get out into the garden and if we did there is a high wall round. What can we do? Please do think of some way to save us."

Jinky showed the note to everyone, and the village held a meeting about it. "Now, we must all think hard," said Jinky. "Shut your eyes, everyone, and think."

They were sitting there with their eyes shut when they heard a bang. It made them jump. They all opened their eyes and gazed round. A little elf called Tricky was trying his hardest not to laugh. Jinky pounced on him.

"Was it you that made that bang? What was it? You naughty elf, making us all jump like that!"

"Please, Jinky, it was only a firework," said Tricky, trying to wriggle away. "It's Guy Fawkes' Day soon, you know, and I've got some fireworks. Humans have them on Firework Night, so I didn't see why I shouldn't have some, too."

Jinky shook the elf hard and he cried. But then an idea slipped into Jinky's mind and he dropped the little elf and began to think about it.

103

"I say!" he said at last. "I say, I've got an idea! I don't know if it will work. But if it does it will get the missing pixies out into the goblin's garden – and with a bit of luck, right over the wall, too!"

"What's your idea?" cried everyone, excited. "Tell us, Jinky."

"Well," said Jinky, "we'll send a fine big box of fireworks to the green goblin. I don't expect he'll know what they are, so the pixies will tell him. They can offer to set them off for him – and when the rockets go flying up into the air they can go with them high over the wall!"

"Oh! What a very, very good idea!" said Dame Shuffle.

"Couldn't be better," said Old Man Spectacles.

"We'll try it!" said Mother Bonnet. "But we must send a message by the mouse to tell the pixies what we are doing. Then they will know what they must do, too."

So they sent a note by the mouse:

104

"The green goblin will receive a present of fireworks. You can explain what they are and offer to set them off in the garden. Hold on to the rockets and ride up into the air with them. You will soon be over the wall and back again with us!"

When the three pixies got this note they were very excited. They kept an eye on the green goblin's post, and one day they saw him with a big brown paper parcel. "What is that, Master?" asked Hoho.

105

The green goblin pulled off the paper and string. He stared at the gaily-covered lid of the box and then he opened the box.

"What are these?" he said, in surprise, when he saw the collection of squibs, catherine wheels, Roman candles, rockets and other things.

"Fireworks for Firework Night," said Hoho. "Surely you have heard of Firework Night, Goblin? It is a night of bangs and pops and bonfires

106

everywhere. It is really a treat belonging to the world of humans, but some of us Little Folk like to share it too."

"But what happens to these things?" said the goblin, picking up a rocket.

"Be careful!" shouted Hoho, making the goblin drop the rocket in alarm. "Unless you know how to use those fireworks you may damage yourself. Be careful!"

"When is Firework Night?" asked the goblin.

"Tomorrow," said Pippy. "How I wish we were going to be at home, and set off fireworks and light a bonfire."

"Oh – do you know how to set these things off then?" asked the goblin, eagerly. "You shall set them going for me tomorrow night."

"But you won't let us go out into the garden," said Tickles. "We can't let them off indoors."

"Well, I'll let you go out tomorrow night," said the goblin. "But I shall put magic into the high wall so that none of you can climb it and escape!"

"We shan't try to climb it," said Hoho, and winked slyly at the other two pixies. "We'll just have fun setting off the fireworks. You can watch from the window, Master. You'll be quite safe indoors!"

So the next night the three pixies hurried out into the garden with the fireworks, and plenty of matches. "We'll set off the catherine wheels first," said Hoho. "They will please the goblin. Then the Roman candles. Then some coloured fire."

So they began. The wheels whizzed round like circles of flame, and the goblin cheered. He liked the Roman candles, too, though he jumped when they began, and almost ran to hide himself under the bed.

He thought everything was wonderful. He kept knocking on the window and shouting, "More! More!"

"Now for the rockets," said Tickles. "Here they are. Almost as big as we are ourselves. Now see what I'm going to

do. I'll put a big one here with its stick in the ground. And another one over here. And the third one here."

"Shall we each go to one and hold it?" asked Hoho.

"Yes. I'll come and light yours first, Pippy," said Tickles. "Then yours, Hoho. And when you have both flown safely up into the air, I'll light my own and follow you. Now, don't be frightened when the rocket bursts into stars. Keep hold of the stick and let it take you safely over the wall, up into the air, and then down to the ground outside!"

He did just as he said. First he lit Pippy's rocket and up it went with a

terrific **WHOOOOSH!** Then he lit Hoho's, and up went that pixie too.

And then he lit his own.

WHOOOOSH! He flew up as well, and the watching goblin cheered and yelled. Each rocket burst into a great shower of coloured stars.

After that there was silence. No more fireworks. No more bangs and pops. No more shouts from the pixies in the garden. They were not there!

The goblin got bored. He threw up the window. "Get on with the fireworks! What's the matter with you? There are plenty more rockets."

There was no answer. In a rage the goblin ran out into the garden. There was nobody there! He hunted everywhere with his big lantern, but the pixies had gone. Where? How? It was the biggest puzzle the green goblin had ever known.

He caught sight of a big glare down in the village. Good gracious, whatever could it be? Was a house on fire?

He hurried down to the village to see. It was, of course, the bonfire built to burn the guy – and you can imagine what guy the villagers were burning! Yes, it was a green goblin guy, of course, as like the real goblin as one pea is to another.

Before he reached the bonfire, what did the goblin see but the three pixies dancing about like mad, overjoyed at being free once more! They had fallen to earth outside the wall, with the rocket sticks, and had scampered down to the village to join the fun.

The goblin gave a roar. "Hi, you! Come back to my castle at once!"

There was a howl of fright from everyone. The goblin ran after the three pixies and came up to the bonfire. What was that sitting in a chair in the middle of the flames, burning away merrily?

The green goblin stared at the guy in dismay. "It's me! I'm in that chair in the flames! They're burning me, the green goblin! Oh! Oh, I'll soon be burnt to nothing! Let me go, let me go!"

"He thinks he's the goblin in the fire!

He thinks he's looking at himself!" goggled Hoho. "Run, green goblin, run! Before you're burnt to bits!"

The green goblin ran. How he ran! You couldn't see his legs, he ran so fast. He didn't stop running till he got to the Land of Goodness Knows Where, and there he stayed. He looked at himself all over. Was he burnt? Was he all right? He'd never, never go back to that pixie village again!

He didn't. So the pixies took the castle for their own, and they give parties in it whenever anyone has a birthday. When is yours? Let them know and maybe they'll send you an invitation!

Stand On
Your Own Feet

Peter was the boy next door. He was eleven years old, strong and jolly, and always laughing. Ann liked him very much.

Ann was ten, but was small for her age. People thought she was eight. She was shy and timid, and she was so afraid of being scolded for anything, that she never owned up when she was in the wrong.

She sat on the wall and watched Peter shooting arrows at a target. "Come and have a try!" said Peter; so she slid down and took the big bow.

"Oh dear – it's so big. It won't spring back and hurt me, will it?"

"Aren't you a little coward!" said Peter, laughing. "Of course it won't.

Look – do it like this."

It was fun playing with Peter. They took turns at shooting arrows at the target; and then suddenly Ann shot one that went right over the wall ! There was a loud miaow and the next-door cat leapt high in the air. The arrow had hit it!

"Oh! Poor thing!" said Peter, and he was over the wall in a flash. But the cat, full of terror, ran away limping. Peter knew he couldn't catch it. He went back over the wall.

"We'd better go round and knock at Miss Milner's door and tell her you hit the cat by accident," said Peter.

Ann stared at him in the greatest alarm.

What! Go and own up to old Miss Milner, who had a very cross face indeed? Why, she wouldn't know a thing about the cat if nobody told her. So why tell her?

"We don't need to say *anything*," said Ann. "She would never know it was one of our arrows that hit her cat. And I don't expect the cat's hurt much,

116

anyway. Miss Milner is *terribly* fierce, you know."

Peter looked fierce, too, quite suddenly. He stared scornfully at Ann.

"Do you know what you are? You're a cowardy custard! Afraid of owning up! The cat *might* be badly hurt – we don't know – and we ought to tell about it. We didn't do it on purpose. Miss Milner will know it was an accident."

"Oh, but, Peter, she'll be so *cross*," said Ann, her eyes filling with tears.

"And what does that matter?" said Peter, still in his horrid, scornful voice. "Have people never been cross with you? Why shouldn't they be sometimes? I feel very cross with you myself. I know it's horrid when people are cross, but even if we don't like it we needn't be *afraid* of it."

"You come with me then, Peter," wept Ann. "*You* tell Miss Milner. And oh, couldn't you say it was *your* arrow that hit the cat? I always feel so scared when things like this happen. You're big and brave, and you're a boy. I'm a

117

girl, and Mummy says I'm timid and sensitive."

"Timid and sensitive!" said Peter sneeringly. "That's what people often say when their children are cowardly and deceitful. Pooh! You're only a year younger than I am, and what does it matter if you're a girl? I've got a cousin of nine called Jean – and she's as brave as anything. She's coming to stay soon, and I'll be glad to have her. She can stand on her own feet – *you* always want to stand on somebody else's."

"I don't, I don't," sobbed Ann, thinking that Peter was very unkind.

"You do," said Peter. "When you got into trouble at school you asked your mother to put it right for you instead of taking your punishment properly. And when you broke Lucy's ruler in half you were afraid to tell her. You got George to explain about it to Lucy. And now you want *me* to go and tell Miss Milner that *I* shot the arrow at the cat. Why can't you stand on your own feet?"

Ann didn't answer. She wiped her eyes and sniffed.

"You'll grow up into a milk-and-water, namby-pamby, weak and silly person," went on Peter. "My mother says people like that have never learned to stand on their own feet and face up to things."

Ann began to cry again. "You don't like me! You won't want to play with me any more."

Peter looked at Ann and felt sorry for her – but not *too* sorry! No, that would never do. He took her arm and shook it gently.

"Ann! I'm going to tell you something

119

nice now. I do like you. You're fun to play with; and if you'd be brave and stand on your own feet *always*, I'd like you as much as I like anyone. But if you don't stand on your own feet I shan't be friends with you at all. You won't be worth it!"

Ann sniffed again, then wiped her eyes and put away her hanky. She looked at Peter, so straight and tall and fearless. She would never, never be like him – but she could at least *try*. She didn't want him to think Jean was wonderful and play only with her when she came to stay with him. It would be horrid to be left out because she was feeble and silly, and a coward.

"I think you've said worse things than any grown-up would say," she told him. "But I think perhaps you're right. I don't believe I ever do stand on my own feet. You watch me now!"

And to Peter's enormous surprise she went out of his garden and up the front path to Miss Milner's house, where she knocked on the door.

When she heard footsteps along the hallway inside she almost ran away. This was the very first time Ann had ever owned up to anything by herself; and although she had felt very brave when she had spoken to Peter, she didn't feel at all brave now.

The door opened – and there stood the cross-faced Miss Milner. "What do you want?" she said.

Ann could hardly get the words out, she was so afraid. "Please – quite by accident – I hit your cat with an arrow. I thought I'd better tell you – in case she was hurt. I'm so sorry."

Ann stammered all this out with a very red face, and then turned to run away. But Miss Milner caught hold of her arm.

"Wait!" she said. "Let's have a look at the cat. She's in the kitchen. How *nice* of you to tell me. Most children wouldn't have said a word."

Ann's heart was still beating fast as she went with Miss Milner into her kitchen. The cat was there in front of the fire. Miss Milner examined her.

"She has a little lump on this leg, but that's all," she said. "I don't think she's hurt much. Thank you for telling me. I think a lot of you for that – and when I see your mother I shall tell her what a

brave little girl she's got, to come and own up like this."

"Peter made me," said Ann, going red again. "I was afraid to."

"Well, here are biscuits for you both," said Miss Milner, reaching up for a tin. "I made them myself. That boy Peter is a good lad – absolutely trustworthy. He'll make a fine man, there's no doubt about that!"

She gave Ann the biscuits and smiled at her. Ann was astonished. Why, Miss Milner hadn't a cross face after all! She thanked her and raced back to Peter, her face glowing. They munched the biscuits together whilst Ann told all that had happened.

"There you are, you see – as soon as you stand on your own feet things aren't nearly so frightening as you think," said Peter. "But, mind you, even if they *are* frightening it's still no reason for not facing up to them. I must say I never thought you had it in you, Ann, to own up like that!"

Ann thought about many things that night in bed. She remembered a lot, too. She remembered how she had once broken one of the panes in the garden shed and hadn't owned up and Daddy thought it was the odd-job boy who had done it. She remembered how she had got into trouble at school over forgotten homework and had begged her mother to go and tell her teacher she hadn't been well and that was why the work wasn't done. And, oh dear, Mother had done what Ann wanted; perhaps Mother didn't know it was wrong not to let her stand on her own feet.

Ann remembered other things. Mother was always making excuses for

her. She wouldn't let Daddy scold her
when she had broken his fountain-pen.
She wouldn't let Granny be cross with
her when Ann had left the tap running
in the basin and flooded the floor. She
hadn't even made Ann go and tell
Granny herself – Mother had gone to
tell her and explain.

"I've been standing on other people's
feet for ages," thought Ann, feeling
ashamed. "It's going to be hard to
stand on my own now. I hope they'll

bear my weight!"

That made her smile. She thought of Peter. However afraid he might be, he always seemed strong and brave and sensible. She wanted him to think well of her. She fell asleep making up her mind that she would be far, far better than his wonderful cousin Jean!

Well, it wasn't easy to keep her word to Peter. All kinds of things happened that seemed to make things as difficult as possible.

She lost one of her exercise books on the way to school, and because she knew she would have to stay in at playtime and get a few sharp words from her teacher she simply could *not* tell her.

She kept thinking what to say and then not saying it. In despair she went to Peter between lessons and told him.

"I'm a coward after all," she said. "I simply *can't* own up!"

"Now you go straight away this minute and say 'Miss Brown, I'm sorry. I must have dropped my exercise book on the way to school'," said Peter. "Go on. This very minute. The more you think of it the worse it will be. It's best to do these things AT ONCE."

Peter was right, of course. It was always best to face up to things at once and get them over. Miss Brown wasn't even cross! She put her hand into her desk – and brought out Ann's exercise book. "Here it is," she said. "Somebody picked it up and brought it to me. Put your name in it, you know that's the rule."

Ann felt so relieved. How silly she had been to worry herself all the morning! If only she had gone to Miss Brown at once.

The next day she broke one of Mother's vases. Ann was horrified. Still, she knew how to get round Mother. She would wait till Mother found the vase, then she would say she

had meant to tell her, and she would cry – and Mother wouldn't scold at all!

"You coward!" Ann said to herself when she had thought all this. "Horrid, deceitful little coward! Go at once and tell Mother."

And she went. Mother was upset, and told Ann she was careless.

"Yes," said Ann. "I *was* careless. Let me buy you another vase out of my own money, Mother."

That made Mother feel very pleased. Ann suddenly felt pleased herself. How nice it was to stand on your own feet! You really did think more of yourself. She felt quite ten centimetres taller!

Then Daddy was quite cross because Ann had left her bicycle out in the rain. Usually she would have run to Mother and cried and asked her to tell Daddy she hadn't meant to – but not this time.

"Daddy, I'm sorry," she said. "I absolutely forgot my bike. I'll dry it and clean it this evening. It won't happen again."

129

Her father looked at her in surprise. Usually Ann wept buckets of tears, and made all kinds of excuses. This was a new Ann, an Ann he liked very much.

"Spoken like a brave lass!" he said, and Ann went red with pleasure.

Still, things weren't easy at all, because it does take a long time to learn to stand on your own feet when you've been using someone else's for ten years! Ann was often afraid, often quite in despair when things went wrong, and she had to somehow summon up enough courage to face them all by herself. She was determined not to ask Mother or Daddy or Peter to help her in anything. It must be her own feet she stood on and nobody else's!

Everyone noticed the change in Ann. Only Peter understood it. He was pleased and proud. Proud of himself because he had made Ann into a nicer person, and proud of Ann for being able to find courage to do it.

And then, just before Peter's cousin

Jean was due to arrive, something else happened. Ann was out on her bicycle, riding some way behind a small boy. Suddenly a dog ran out and collided with the back wheel of the boy's bicycle. Off he fell at once and lay in the road, squealing with fright and pain.

And what did Ann do? She didn't do what she would have done three weeks before – screamed and ridden away as fast as she could.

No – she rode up to the boy, shooed away the big playful dog, helped up the screaming child, and took him into the nearest house to have his cut knees seen to. She found out his name and address and went riding off to tell his mother and to ask her to come and fetch him home.

Peter heard about it because the boy's mother was a great friend of his own mother's, and told her all about Ann. "A more sensible, helpful child I never saw!" said the little boy's mother. "Stood on her own feet, and did all the right things at once. Now, I do like a child like that."

Peter was bursting with pride. He rushed off to tell Ann. She went red and looked away. She was so pleased to hear Peter's praise that she couldn't say a word.

"I'm glad you're my friend," said Peter. "You really are a friend to be proud of."

"It's a pity Jean's coming tomorrow," said Ann with a sigh. "Just as I'm getting sensible enough to be your friend. Now you'll have Jean and you won't want anyone else to play with."

"Jean will like you awfully," said Peter. "Come and play every day, will you? We'll go for picnics together and go swimming. It'll be fun, the three of us."

It *is* fun. Ann's having a lovely time. She always stands on her own feet now, and what I would dearly like to know is – do you?

Silly
Sammy

Sammy was a silly little boy. When anyone teased him, he believed them, and cried. Jimmy told him there were dragons in the garden, and he went in to his mother, wailing loudly.

"It's only the snapdragons," said Jimmy. "Don't be such a baby, Sammy."

Another day Lisa told him she had seen the moon shining at her from the waters of the duck-pond the night before.

"Oh! Has the moon fallen out of the sky into the duck-pond, then?" asked Sammy, in surprise. "Mummy! Mummy, where are you? Lisa says the moon fell out of the sky last night. Oh, Mummy, the sun won't fall, will it? Oh, I feel frightened!"

Now Sammy's mother was rather silly. Instead of laughing at Sammy and saying "What a little silly you are! Just think a minute and you'll know what Lisa means!" she would put her arms round him and comfort him. She would say: "Poor darling little Sammy! Did the other children tease you? Never mind, darling, Mummy loves you!"

And that made Sammy more of a baby than ever, of course. It's good to have a mother who will comfort us at the right time, but it's bad when we're being silly!

Now one day Sammy trod on a spider without meaning to. He stood looking down at his feet, sorry for the little squashed creature. Lisa nudged Jimmy.

"Let's tease him," she said. It wasn't very kind of her but poor Sammy was so very, very teasable.

"Oooh!" said Lisa, in a shocked voice. "You've killed a spider. You'll have awful bad luck now. You'll break all your toys. You'll lose your money. You'll get into trouble at school."

136

Sammy stared at her in horror. "Shall I really?" he said, and his eyes filled with tears. "What else will happen to me?"

"I'll tell you," said naughty Lisa, and she giggled at Jimmy nearby. "Your feet will grow *big*, and everyone will know you've killed a spider."

"How big?" said poor Sammy, a tear trickling down his cheek.

"Oooh, I don't know," said Lisa. "Big as a giant's, maybe. You *will* look funny!"

"I'm going home to Mummy," said Sammy. He turned to go, and Lisa called after him:

"Don't forget your goloshes. Wait, I'll bring them."

She ran to where the goloshes were kept, but instead of taking out Sammy's goloshes, she took out her own small ones. She ran to Sammy, trying not to laugh. Sammy had very big feet indeed!

"Here you are," she said. "Put them on quickly."

Sammy sat down and tried to pull one on over his shoe. It simply wouldn't go on at all. He tried and he tried.

"It's funny," he said. "My golosh won't go on. Bother!"

"I expect your feet are getting bigger already," said Lisa solemnly. "Poor Sammy. Goodness, if they've grown out of your goloshes so soon, they will be as big as boats this evening."

"Oh! Oh! My feet are growing bigger!" wept Sammy. "What shall I do? What shall I *do*?"

"Try the other golosh," said Jimmy. But that wouldn't go on either, which was not at all surprising, as Lisa's goloshes were two sizes smaller than

Sammy's! The silly little boy wailed loudly, got up and ran home as fast as he could go, leaving the goloshes behind.

"Mummy! Mummy!" he yelled, going into the house. "Oh, Mummy! A dreadful thing is happening!"

But his mother was not there, only his father, who didn't at all approve of Sammy's silliness. He liked a boy to *be* a boy and not a baby.

"What's happening?" he asked.

"Daddy! My feet are growing bigger and bigger," wailed Sammy.

"Of course they are. Children's feet

are always growing," said his father. "Don't be silly."

"But Daddy, you don't understand," wailed Sammy. "I trod on a spider, and now awful things will happen to me! Really they will. One of them is that my feet will grow bigger and bigger, and they'll be as big as boats this evening. I tried to put on my goloshes, and I couldn't. They were too small."

Sammy's mother came in, and when she saw Sammy crying and wailing, she held out her arms to him.

"No," said Sammy's father. "Don't make a fuss of him, please. He's being so very, very silly, that I really think it's time he was stopped. He is actually telling me that because he trod on a spider his feet are getting big! Can any child be quite so silly as to believe that?"

"Lisa said so, Lisa said so," wept silly Sammy.

"Oh, the naughty girl!" said Sammy's mother. But Sammy's father shook his head.

"If anyone is so babyish as Sammy, I don't really blame Lisa for teasing him," he said.

"I don't like being teased!" wailed Sammy.

"Stop that noise," said his father. "You are teased because you behave like a baby and don't use your brains. Stop crying."

But Sammy didn't stop. His father looked at him. "I think what he wants is a good smack," he said, solemnly. "That might make him see sense."

Sammy stopped wailing at once, as if by magic. His father looked at him sternly. "Go and fetch your other shoes, and your boots, and your bedroom slippers," he said. "We'll soon see if your feet are growing big."

142

Sammy went to fetch them. His father made him take off his shoes and try on the boots, shoes and slippers.

"If your feet have grown, then none of these will fit you," he said. "It seems an extraordinary thing, doesn't it, that the shoes you came home in should have grown too? I don't believe they have. Anyway, try on all these boots and shoes at once."

Sammy did – and of course they all fitted him perfectly. It seemed most astonishing to him.

"Now go back to Lisa's and fetch your goloshes," said his father. So off went Sammy. Lisa gave him his own

goloshes this time, and to his enormous surprise they went over his own shoes easily.

"My feet must have gone back to their right size then," said Sammy, puzzled.

"Well, you didn't kill the spider after all," said Lisa. "It uncurled all its legs and ran off after you'd gone. So I suppose your feet went back to their right size again."

Sammy believed her. He ran off happily to tell his father.

"Oh, what a little silly you are!" said

his father, with a sigh. "I suppose you didn't think that Lisa might have given you the wrong goloshes at first, did you? She is just as clever as you are silly! Now, Sammy – what about stopping this nonsense, and being a big boy?"

"I'll try and remember," said Sammy, going red when he thought of how Lisa and Jimmy must have laughed at him when he tried on the wrong goloshes, and thought his feet had grown big all of a sudden.

"Listen, I'll always say, 'Sammy, be careful your feet don't grow big' to remind you when I think you're going to be silly," said his father. "You'll soon remember!"

Well, the first day his father said it to him twenty three times, the second day fifteen times, the third day twelve times, the fourth day nine times, and the fifth day three times. So it rather looks as if he's being cured, doesn't it?

I shan't bother to say it to *you*! I'm sure you don't behave like Silly Sammy.

They Wouldn't Be
Friends With Him

Prince Kirrion felt very pleased with himself. He meant to run away for the whole afternoon and have a good time – and it looked as if he would be able to do exactly what he had planned.

He was lying in bed. The curtains were pulled across the windows to keep out the bright afternoon sun. His governess had tiptoed out of the room after telling him she wouldn't disturb him until five o'clock.

"Poor little prince!" she said. "Such a nasty thing to have a bad headache. You must have been out in the sun too much. You were a good boy to tell me so that I could pop you into bed to get you better."

Prince Kirrion grinned to himself

when he thought of all she had said. As soon as the door was safely shut he leaned on his elbow and looked round the room. There were his clothes put neatly on a chair – but he wasn't going to wear those. No – he had a suit of clothes hidden safely away in a drawer, a suit that he had taken out of someone else's room. It belonged to one of the king's pages.

Kirrion was eleven years old, and he thought the world of himself. His mother thought the world of him, too. His father didn't see him very often because he was king and had a great deal to do. He was pleased, though, that Kirrion was good-looking, strong and clever.

Kirrion was bored with life in the palace. He didn't like Dame Rosalind, his governess, and he disliked his tutor, too.

"He shouldn't make me work so hard!" thought Kirrion sulkily. "As if it matters whether a king knows how to spell properly or not! He's always got somebody to do his spelling for him, hasn't he? It's a waste of my time to bother about spelling and tables. I want to go out into the world and do the things other boys and girls do."

He often thought of the other children he saw from his carriage when he went riding. Sometimes the boys were fishing in the stream. Sometimes they were picnicking by the field-side.

Often they were playing cricket or football on the greens. They shouted and laughed and chased one another. Kirrion wanted to do all that, too.

And now he was really going to! He had got this suit of clothes by a very clever trick, and he had told Dame Rosalind that he had a bad headache and wanted to rest until it went. Now he was going to dress himself in the suit of clothes, steal downstairs to the larder and take some food, then slip out by the garden gate to find someone to go picnicking with him.

"I'm very clever," thought Prince Kirrion. "Nobody dreams how clever I am! Whilst they all think I'm lying here with a headache I shall be out in the countryside with a basket of food, making all kinds of new friends. How

149

proud people will be to be friends with a prince!"

It was a hot spring day. Kirrion got out of bed and listened. No one was about. Most people were in their rooms, resting after a long meeting in the council hall that morning. It was just the time to slip out now.

Kirrion dressed in the suit of clothes he had taken from the little page's chest of drawers. It was the boy's home suit, a plain brown tunic and short knickerbockers, with long stockings and brown leather sandals. Kirrion thought he looked very ordinary and plain in them. He was used to wearing very grand clothes indeed.

He slipped out of his room and ran quickly to the back stairs. He went down them cautiously. He stood at the bottom and listened. Most of the servants had gone to watch the first cricket match of the season on the nearby green. One or two were still left, and Kirrion could hear them talking in the big pantry.

There was no one in the kitchen. He slipped in and ran to the larder. He quickly stuffed all kinds of things into a big basket. What a fine picnic he would have with whatever new friends he found!

Then out he went into the garden and down to the old gate in the wall. He was soon standing in the lane, full of delight. Now his adventure was beginning!

He made his way into the nearby wood. He had meant to walk for miles right away from the palace, but he soon felt tired. He wished he could meet some other children. Where could they have gone to this afternoon?

151

He sat down to rest under a tree. All round him were big clumps of yellow primroses. It was a nice place to rest in.

A little dog came running up to him, panting. It licked his face, and Kirrion was cross. "Get away, I tell you, or I'll throw a stone at you!"

"Don't you dare!" said a girl's voice, and a little girl of about Kirrion's age came round a tree. "All dogs lick. What's the harm in that?"

Then a boy came along, too. He was a bit older than Kirrion. The little prince was pleased to see them both, though he felt cross at being spoken to so sharply by the girl.

"What are you doing in the wood?" asked Kirrion, remembering to be polite.

"Picking primroses for Mother," said the little girl. "We haven't any in our garden at all."

"Well, let's dig some up, then," said Kirrion at once. "Oh–there's nothing to dig with. Well, let's pull up some roots, then." He tugged at a big primrose clump and up it came.

"Don't do that," said the little girl, shocked. "People can pick flowers in woods, but it's wrong to dig up the whole plant. Why, if everyone did that there would soon be no flowers left to pick."

"Pooh! Take what you want," said Kirrion. "That's what I always do." He tugged at another primrose root. The

153

little girl stopped him. "Don't, please. We shan't take them home, because our mother wouldn't like us to steal them from the wood."

Kirrion tugged harder. The boy spoke; his voice was so commanding that Kirrion obeyed. "Leave the primroses alone! Do you hear?"

The prince felt nervous. Nobody ever spoke to him like that! He remembered the picnic basket. The children would be friends with him if he shared his food with them. He pulled everything out of the basket.

"Come and picnic with me," he begged them. "Look – here's a whole roast chicken – and look at this lovely pie! And did you ever see such nice jam tarts? There's this cream cake, too. Let's all share."

The boy and girl looked in amazement at the rich food.

"Where did you get that from?" asked the boy. "Why, that's food fit for a king!"

That made Kirrion laugh heartily.

"That's a good joke!" he said. "It was meant to be food for a king – the king himself! I crept into the palace larder and took it for a picnic meal. What do you think of that?"

"I think you're a dreadful storyteller," said the little girl. "Really dreadful. I'm quite sure you've never been inside the palace! And if you did take that food from the larder, you're a thief!"

"You're a nasty girl," said Kirrion angrily. "And I'll just tell you this: I'm the prince of this country – Prince Kirrion!"

He quite expected the children to
kneel down before him and beg his
pardon. But they didn't. They laughed
scornfully.

"Storyteller!" said the girl. "Silly,
stupid storyteller!"

"I tell you it's true," said Kirrion, red
with rage. "Why shouldn't it be? Is it
because I've got on plain brown
clothes? Well, I took these out of a

drawer in one of the pages' rooms. He didn't know anything about it. I was too clever! I expect he got into trouble for losing it."

"Why do you make yourself out to be so horrid?" said the boy. "Do you really think these things are clever?"

"I'm not horrid!" cried Kirrion, and leapt to his feet. "Look here – I'm the prince himself. I told my silly old governess I'd got a headache and wanted to go to bed. But as soon as she left me I got into these clothes, took this food out of the larder, and came into these woods to find some children for friends, to share a picnic with me. Why don't you believe me? Don't I *look* like a prince?"

"No," said the little girl. "You've got a mean face, for one thing. And you tell stories and steal things, for another. Princes don't behave like that. The king of this country is a fine man. I've often heard my father say so. He wouldn't have a son like you, I'm sure. You're just a fraud."

The little prince was so angry that he could hardly think of a word to say. He roared with rage and stamped around among the primroses. The other two watched him and laughed. He couldn't bear that.

He picked up the roast chicken and threw it at the little girl. He threw the meat-pie at the boy.

Suddenly he felt two strong hands on his arms. He felt a hard slap on his face. He found himself on his back, with somebody tying up his hands.

It was the boy. "I'll show you what happens to kids who hurt my sister!" the boy was saying fiercely. "You'll be tied up to this tree until you say you're sorry, you mean, bad-tempered, boastful little fellow!"

With tears of rage pouring down his cheeks, Kirrion was soon tied to a small tree. The boy and the girl stood looking at him. "Prince, indeed!" said the boy scornfully. "More likely you're the son of somebody put in prison for doing bad things. That's where you'll be put, too, one of these days! Now, just say you're sorry!"

"I shan't say I'm sorry, I shan't, I shan't!" wept Kirrion, struggling to get free. "I'll stay here for weeks and weeks before I say I'm sorry. You've insulted the prince. You'll both be punished for this!"

"Come on. Let's leave him there," said the boy. "We'll come back after tea and see if he's learnt any sense."

So they left him and went home. They had their tea, and went back to the wood where they had left Kirrion. But on the way they heard the sound of horses' hoofs. Along came a big man on horseback, followed by six others. They reined in their horses when they saw the two children.

"Have you seen a boy in prince's clothing?" the first horseman asked.

160

"No," said the little girl. "We met a stupid boy in the woods who said he was the prince, but he wasn't. He was very rude and silly, and we tied him up."

"Tell me about it," said the horseman. The boy told him all that had happened.

"He actually dared to say he was the prince," he finished. "But no prince would behave like that, so we didn't believe him. And when he threw things at my little sister and hurt her I slapped him, knocked him down and tied him up. We're just on our way to him now. If he says he's sorry we'll let him go."

"Just fancy! He wanted us to be friends with him and have a picnic," said the little girl. "As if we would be friends with a boy like that!"

"I'll come with you," said the horseman, and he signed to the other riders to stop where they were. He leapt off his horse, left it and went with the children.

"I'll just keep behind a tree," he said. "I want to see this bad boy. You go and talk to him."

The two children were puzzled by the big horseman. What had happened? Why was he looking for a boy dressed in prince's clothing? Surely he couldn't be looking for that silly boy they had tied up?

They came to the tree where they had tied up the prince. He was crying with fright. "Let me go, let me go! I'm sorry! I won't do it again. I'm frightened of being here alone. Let me go!"

"Are you sorry you pulled up the primroses by their roots?" demanded the little girl. "Are you sorry you told such stories? Are you sorry you threw things at us, and lost your temper?"

"Yes, I'm sorry, I'm sorry," wept Kirrion. "But I didn't tell you stories. I *am* the prince. I did give my governess the slip. I did take those things out of the larder, and I did take this suit from one of the pages at the palace."

"Silly!" said the little girl. The boy went to untie the prince from the tree. As soon as he was free Kirrion turned on them.

"You horrid children! You think you can do these things to me, the prince! I'll show you what happens to people who do that to me! I'll have you punished! I'll have you locked up with nothing but bread and water. I'll ... I'll..."

"Kirrion," said a stern voice, and from behind the tree stepped the big horseman. Kirrion knew him at once and trembled.

"Your Majesty, my father!" he whispered.

The other two children went pale and knelt down before the king.

"Get up," said the king. "It is my son who should kneel to us, not you to me. Little did I think that I would find in two strange children all the good things that are missing in my own son! Kirrion, you shall have the punishment you planned to give to these two children. You will be locked up for two days on bread and water."

"Oh, don't punish him," said the little girl. "He's so frightened now."

"So you are kind as well as good!" said the king. "What a pity my son hasn't friends like you!"

"I want them for my friends," wept the prince. "I like them. My father, Your Majesty, may they be my friends and come to the palace?"

"We will see," said the king, and took Kirrion away.

"I hope we shall never see the king again," said the little girl to her brother that night. "He might be angry with us next time."

But they did see him again, many times, and they grew to love him. He sent for them to play with Kirrion, and to have lessons with him.

"You can teach him far more than any governess or tutor!" he told them. "Do your best!" It was a very good best. Kirrion grew up into a king as fine as his father – but he has never forgotten how it happened.

"It all began that day I ran into the woods," he said. "What a good thing you two laughed at me and tied me up."

And I really think it was.

Sally
Simple's Mistake

It was a blowy, blustery April day when Sally Simple set out to go and call on her Aunt Amanda. She had to hold on to her hat tightly, or it would have flown straight off her head.

"Oh, dear, oh, dear – what a wind!" said poor Sally, struggling along, her skirts blowing this way and that. She put down her hand to pat her skirts straight – and at once her hat flew right off her head!

"Look at that now!" said Sally. She turned to watch the hat bowling along. "All those pretty flowers getting muddy and wet – and the brim getting bent. And I did so badly want to look nice for Aunt Amanda. She is so very particular!"

She went after her hat. It was lying

in a puddle. She shook the water from it and it flew all over her. "I can't wear it any more!" she wailed. "It's spoilt!"

She tucked it under her arm and struggled on again. She felt drops of rain on her head – now it was going to rain hard and soak her through!

The rain came down in bucketfuls. Sally had an umbrella with her, and she shook it out ready to put up. She opened it – and immediately the wind took it and turned it inside out!

Sally could have cried. First her hat spoilt and now her nice umbrella blown inside out. Bother the wind! She put her ruined umbrella under her arm with her hat and walked on again.

When she got to the corner of the lane the wind rushed at her with such strength that she was blown backwards – and down she went on the wet grass at the edge of the lane.

She sat there to get her breath – and then she suddenly saw something by her knee. Why – it was a four-leaved clover! Fancy that!

"A four-leaved clover!" cried Sally Simple. "Now, there's a bit of luck! Anybody knows a four-leaved clover is lucky. And I need good luck, too, after all the bad luck I've had this morning with my hat and my umbrella!"

She picked the clover carefully and put it into her bag. Now she would really be lucky. What a pity she hadn't found it before her hat and umbrella had been spoilt.

She went down the lane, on the way to her aunt's, shaking her hat every now and again, hoping it would be all right to wear. But she was sure it wouldn't. The flowers were muddy and torn, and the brim was wet, and was coming apart in two places.

It began to rain hard again. Sally stepped off the road and went into a little shed to shelter – and there she saw something very surprising indeed!

A hat was hanging on a nail at the back of the shed – and beside it, on another nail, was a neatly-rolled umbrella, striped black and red – really a very nice one indeed.

"Well, now, look there!" said Sally, amazed. "Would you believe it? If that isn't good luck brought by the four-leaved clover already! My, my – I

wonder what else I shall find. This is too good to be true!"

She put the pretty flowery hat on her head, and took down the neat umbrella. She hung up her own spoilt hat and put the inside-out umbrella beside it.

Then off she went, feeling very grand. The rain had stopped, and the wind wasn't quite so blowy. But, all the same, Sally held her new hat on tightly.

Aunt Amanda was very pleased to

see her. "*What* a pretty new hat, Sally!" she said. "Do come in. And my, you've a new umbrella, too, I see. Leave it in the hall. That's right. You go and wait in the sitting-room until I come. I'm just baking a few cakes for tea, because I've a friend coming."

"That *will* be nice," said Sally, happily. "It will be quite a party. If you're sure I can't help you, Aunt Amanda, I'll just go and look round the garden."

Off she went, and spent a nice time looking at the daffodils and wallflowers and primroses. Then she heard voices from the kitchen, and she guessed her aunt's friend must have arrived.

"I'd better go back to the house,"

172

thought Sally. So back she went. As she passed the kitchen window she heard her aunt's voice.

"Well, I never did! Whatever do you mean, Mrs Smart? Somebody stole your hat and umbrella? But how did that happen?"

"Well, I was going along the lane in my best hat with my best umbrella," said the friend's voice loudly, "and I saw a little lamb in the ditch. So I went to lift it through the hedge – and I took off my new hat first, in case the wind should blow it off my head, and hung it in a nearby shed, and I hung up my best umbrella beside it."

"And when you came back they were gone!" said Aunt Amanda, shocked. "You should go to the police, Mrs Smart."

"They were not only gone, but some gipsy or other had left these awful old things in their place," said Mrs Smart, showing Aunt Amanda a dreadful hat, wet and muddy, and an inside-out umbrella. "Did you ever see such

things?"

Sally Simple stood outside the window, shaking at the knees. Oh my, oh my! It wasn't a bit of luck she had had after all: it was just that Mrs Smart had put her hat and umbrella carefully out of the way when she went to get the lamb. And she, Sally, had taken them and put her spoilt ones in their place.

Whatever was she to do? She stole

into the house and took off the smart new hat. She hung it on a peg in the hall, just above where she had stood the neat umbrella.

Her own spoilt hat was there on the peg and the ragged umbrella in a corner nearby. Sally Simple took them with trembling hands.

She must go! Mrs Smart would be so very, very angry if she knew what Sally had done, and Aunt Amanda would never, never forgive her.

"I ought to own up, I know I ought," thought Sally. "But I daren't. Anyway, I'm trying to put things right again. And oh, I know what I'll do! I'll slip my four-leaved clover, my precious four-leaved clover, into the ribbon round Mrs Smart's lovely hat – then she'll get some luck, and I'll have made up to her for being so very silly."

So she put the four-leaved clover into the hat band. Then she stole out of the front door, wearing her wet, raggedy hat, with her inside-out umbrella under her arm.

Poor Sally Simple – it was a pity she didn't stay and own up. Mrs Smart would have laughed and laughed, and so would Aunt Amanda. And she would have had a lovely tea and felt very much better. But she wasn't brave enough.

I wish I were going to be there when Mrs Smart suddenly sees her own hat and umbrella in the hall, don't you? She *will* get a tremendous surprise! Whatever will she say?

No Present
For Benny

Amanda was very happy. It was Christmas Day and she had had a lovely lot of presents. There had been plenty in her stocking, and some more on the breakfast-table. She had had just the things she wanted – a big new baby doll, a fine lot of books, and a new pencil-box full of lovely pencils.

And now they were all getting ready to go to Granny's for Christmas Day dinner. There would be an enormous turkey and a plum-pudding too. Grandpa would carve the turkey and make jokes. Auntie Susan would be there, and she was nice, too.

"There will be six of us at Granny's, won't there?" said Amanda, counting.

"No, eight," said Mummy. "Auntie

Lucy and her little boy, Benny, will be there, too. You remember him, don't you, Amanda? A dear little shy boy."

"Oh, yes. I loved him," said Amanda, thinking of the merry little boy, shy and kind, that she had played with at Auntie Lucy's the summer before. "But oh, Mummy – I've just thought of something dreadful!"

"What?" said her mother, buttoning up Amanda's coat.

"I didn't know Benny was coming – so I haven't got a present for him," said Amanda. "Whatever shall I do?"

"It doesn't matter," said Mummy. "He won't mind. Come along now, we mustn't wait another minute or we shall miss the bus."

Amanda hurried along the road, worrying about having no present for Benny. She liked giving everybody presents. She didn't like missing anyone out. She hadn't known Benny was going, or she would certainly have bought him a present. But now she had spent all her money and she couldn't even buy him one when the shops were open.

Benny was at Granny's, shy and smiling. He ran to Amanda and gave her a hug. And then he held out a parcel to her. "Happy Christmas!" he said. "I've brought a present for you."

"Oh, Benny!" said Amanda, and felt worse than ever. She undid the parcel. Inside was a jigsaw puzzle, just the kind she liked. "Thank you," she said. "You really are kind."

She did wish she had a present for Benny. She thought he looked hurt because she didn't give him one. Amanda worried so much about it that it began to spoil her Christmas Day. Still, it didn't spoil her appetite for her dinner!

The turkey was carved by Grandpa, who made his usual funny jokes. Then came the Christmas pudding. It was a beauty, black as could be.

"I made it myself," said Granny. "I hope it will taste good."

It did. It tasted lovely. But suddenly

Amanda felt her teeth biting on something rather hard. She was puzzled. She took the hard thing out of her mouth and looked at it. It was an old sixpenny piece! "Gosh, look what I've found in my pudding!" she said to Granny.

Granny laughed. "Oh yes – I forgot to remind you all that there are old sixpenny pieces in the pudding. Now, Benny - perhaps you will find one too!"

But Benny didn't. He was very disappointed, because he knew Christmas pudding sixpences were special, lucky ones. And Amanda suddenly bit on something hard again in her very last mouthful – and there was another sixpence!

"You *are* a lucky girl!" said everyone, and Amanda thought she was too. And then, as she looked at the two little sixpences lying on the edge of her plate, a fine idea came to her. She could give them to Benny for a Christmas present! He would like them very much.

So, after dinner, she took her sixpences and washed them. Then she polished them to make them bright. She went to find Benny.

"Benny," she said, "I didn't bring you a present because I didn't know you would be here. But now I've got one for you – my Christmas pudding sixpences! Here you are, and I wish you a happy Christmas!"

"Oh, *thank* you!" said Benny, "but only give me one. You keep one for yourself."

But Amanda wouldn't. She made Benny have them both, and the little boy was delighted. "Do you know," he said, "*no*body gave me any money this Christmas and I do like a little to spend

182

afterwards, don't you, when our money boxes are all empty? Now I shall have Christmas money after all! It's the nicest present you could have given me!"

"I'm glad," said Amanda, feeling very pleased. She danced away, looking happy again. She wasn't worried any more. She had given Benny a present after all!

"I *was* lucky to get two sixpences in the Christmas pudding!" she said to herself.

And she really was, wasn't she?

Betsy-May
in Disgrace

Once Betsy-May behaved very badly
indeed. She went out for a walk with
Nanny, and baby James was in his
pram. Betsy-May didn't want to go out
for a walk. She wanted to stay and play
in the garden.

"No," said Nanny. "You know we
always go out in the afternoon. You can
have the morning to play in the
garden."

"I'm tired," said Betsy-May, and
dragged her feet one after the other, so
that she scraped the toes of her shoes
on the ground and spoilt them.

"Don't do that, Betsy-May," said
Nanny. "See how you are spoiling your
nice shoes. Don't be such a baby."

"I want to ride in the pram," said

184

Betsy-May, in a whiny sort of voice. "My legs are tired."

"If you speak to me in that voice I shall think you are more of a baby than Baby James," said Nanny.

Betsy-May dragged behind. Nanny pulled her to the pram and made her take hold of the handle.

"Look at Baby staring at you!" she said. "He can't make out who you are. You don't look a bit like Betsy-May with that silly face you are making. I really am ashamed of you. Now walk properly, because here is Mary-Jane coming with her nanny."

But Betsy-May would not do as she was told. She wouldn't say "Good

185

afternoon." She turned her back on Mary-Jane and her nanny. She really was very naughty.

"She's behaving like a baby," said Nanny. "I almost think I'll lift James out of the pram and let him toddle, and pop Betsy-May in and wheel her."

Mary-Jane laughed loudly. She thought that was a funny joke. "Yes, do do that," she begged. "I want to see Betsy-May looking like a baby in a pram."

Betsy-May stamped her foot. "I won't be put in the pram," she said. "I won't!"

"Very well," said Nanny. "Then come along and walk properly. Goodbye, Mary-Jane. Good-bye."

But still Betsy-May wouldn't walk nicely. She dragged her feet again, and suddenly she tripped over the kerb and fell down.

She didn't hurt herself. She had the tiniest red mark on her knee, but that was all. All the same, she opened her mouth and yelled so loudly that baby

James was frightened, and he began to cry too.

"Well I never!" said Nanny vexed, because everyone stared at her and the children. "Betsy-May, stop making that noise this minute. I have never known you behave so babyishly before. One more yell from you, and I'll put you straight to bed the minute we get home. You can't be well."

Betsy-May stopped yelling. She knew quite well Nanny would keep her word, and she didn't like going to bed before tea. She was quite well. She was only cross and naughty.

She looked at Nanny's cross face. She didn't like it when Nanny put on that sort of face. It was so different from her ordinary smiling face. Nanny stopped at the toy-shop, lifted out James, and took him inside. Betsy-May went too. Nanny bought James a nice soft ball. But she didn't buy Betsy-May anything.

"I don't buy presents for little girls who behave like babies," she said. She put James back into his pram, and he played with the ball. Then they went to the baker's and Nanny bought a fat sponge-finger for James. But she didn't buy one for Betsy-May, as she usually did.

"I don't buy sponge-fingers for little girls who behave so stupidly," she said.

Betsy-May felt sad. She walked properly. She looked at Nanny, but Nanny didn't look at her once. James made some funny noises and Nanny talked to him. But she didn't talk to Betsy-May. It was dreadful.

"I mustn't cry about it," thought Betsy-May, trying to squeeze back a tear. "If I do, then Nanny will say I'm a baby again. Oh dear, I don't like her to think I'm a baby. She knows that really I am a big little girl, much older than James. She always says I'm a help to her. Now she doesn't love me any more because she thinks I've gone back to being a baby."

They went home. Nanny went to fetch in the clean clothes from the line. Betsy-May stayed in the nursery. The clock struck four. It was nearly tea-time.

"I'm a very big girl!" said Betsy-May, out loud, "I can help grown-up people a lot. I shall get the tea ready."

She got the cloth and spread it over the table. She got the plates, the cups

189

and saucers, and she put out plates for the bread-and-butter and cake. She found the bread in the tin, and the butter, too, nearby.

"That's done," said Betsy-May, pleased. She put the two chairs up to the table, and dragged up Baby James's high chair as well.

Toys had been left on the floor. Betsy-May put them tidily away in the cupboard. Nanny's knitting lay on the seat of her armchair. The cat might come and play with it. Betsy-May put it carefully away in a blue knitting-bag. She fetched Baby James's feeder from the drawer. Then she heard Nanny

190

coming, and she sat on the window-seat, waiting.

Nanny came in, carrying James on her left arm, talking to him merrily. But when she looked at Betsy-May she didn't smile. Then she suddenly saw the tea was laid.

"Who laid the tea?" she said in surprise.

"Well, I did," said Betsy-May.

"Who put out the bread and the butter?" said Nanny.

"I did that too," said Betsy-May.

"Who put the chairs up to the table?" asked Nanny, still astonished.

"I did," said Betsy-May.

"And who tidied away the toys we left out, and put away my knitting, and fetched Baby James's feeder?" said Nanny.

191

"I did it all," said Betsy-May. "I'm not a baby, you see. You were wrong. I'm somebody big who wants to help."

"So you are!" said Nanny, and she smiled her usual smile at Betsy-May. "Now, why ever did I think you were a baby? I've really forgotten. I can see you are a very big and sensible girl. I shall have to tell Mummy all about you. She *will* be pleased!"

She was! Betsy-May had chocolate biscuits for her supper.

"Babies are treated like babies, but big girls are treated like big girls," said Nanny, when she had bathed her. "Just remember that, Betsy-May!"

"Of course I will," said Betsy-May. "It's much nicer to be big."

So it is, isn't it?